CLAIMED BY THE OUTLAW

A Ghosts of Deadwood Romance

USA Today Bestselling Author
Cyndi Faria

"Agnes, darling, if such should be we never meet again, while firing my last shot, I will gently breathe the name of my wife Agnes and with wishes even for my enemies, I will make the plunge and try to swim to the other shore."

~James Butler Hickok (Wild Bill Hickok)

DEDICATION

This book is dedicated to my dad who passed while I was writing. He dreamed of an afterlife filled with adventure and possibilities, of fishing the Mad River for wild steelhead and salmon, of staring out across the Pacific, and hauling crab traps overflowing with Dungeness caught out of Bodega Bay.

I hope you're limiting out every day at your happy places, Dad.

Miss you and love you, Cyn

April 10th 1935 – March 16th, 2020

CHAPTER 1

Agnes "Emily" Lyffe

Remember when we lived? Remember the red brick road, the orange glow of the summer sunset over the Black Hills, the Grille's prosciutto and brie, and Belle Joli's Chablis? Remember laughing until we held our ribs and tears slid down our cheeks? Remember counting stars, naming them, telling me you wished our love would never dim? Remember the clock's hands moved too quickly and we

woke tangled in linen and lace? Remember you promised to meet me at midnight at the place we met every anniversary of that day? I wish I could change the past. I want to. Believe me, Emily. If only I had a second chance, I'd show you a miracle and set us both free.

I huff out a long, exasperated breath at my ex-fiancé's exaggerated message, wondering if Mike drunk texted me again. How many times can he break my heart? Deadwood is my heaven on earth. I thought it was his too. I hoped it could be ours. At least, I had before the accident.

I slam the key into the doorknob of Mom's shop, Deadwood Antiques, but the keys fall into a twisted array at my feet. "Shit, shit, shit."

The damn text messes with my head that's suddenly swimming with an onslaught of memories, which suck me into a vortex and threaten to swallow me on the spot.

I brush back tears of bewilderment and bitterness. This wasn't supposed to be my life. But it is, so I gotta suck it up.

Picking up the cluster of keys, I find a slender, tarnished one that has fit this door for over a hundred years. Twisting the key, I lock the antique shop that once belonged to my mom not so long ago. My heart clenches at the thought of selling, but I have no choice.

Streetlights and storefronts light my path as I slog toward the Bullock Hotel, having to stay somewhere since Mom's home is no longer available. *Sure hope they have a room.* The spring night air nips at my cheeks, urging me to quicken my pace.

More than anything, I want to settle down here and raise a family. But after the accident, after losing my mother and my unborn child, after Mike disappeared, I'm torn, and forgiving him is right up there with bedding down in a cramped den of restless rattlesnakes.

I peek at the text, wondering if our pregnancy was what tied us instead of love.

After three months, I can't understand Mike's sudden change of heart. I admit, the prospect of reconnecting with him intrigues me, but caution warns me not to make the same mistake, agreeing with Mom's dying words to let go.

I swallow back the ache in my throat and the haunting memory of seeing her that last time. I check the text again to see if it's real, but as I stare, I notice the GPS is turned on, letting me know Mike's actually here in Deadwood. At the hotel— *our* hotel—the Bullock Hotel. *WTH, Mike.* I stomp my foot and barely feel anything. I'm numb feet to brows. And I will be until I resolve my anger.

Until I confront Mike.

However, moving on feels impossible as his recollection of our time together wakes my memories, reminding me of the happiest moments of my life. I glance at the text for the last time, and an unexpected feeling of hope nudges me onward.

But hope for what? Rekindling our relationship, simply calling a truce, acknowledging we tried and failed, or giving myself permission to move on? Date? Find a new way to get what I want?

It's dinner hour, and the streets pack with tourists during Wild Bill Days. I dart around couples holding hands, snuggling against each other, laughing, canoodling. It's all too much when I long for the type of deep connection they each have, but at the same time, I'm jaded by my experiences in the love department. True love doesn't exist.

Winded by the time I push through the crush of people, when I get to the hotel, I can't let the door close behind me quick enough as I catch my breath.

The interior is a wash of burgundy and green, furniture that clings to a period long overdue for an update, some would say. I find the decor reminds me of home, of history, of tradition. Bully's

Restaurant is just as I remember: welcoming and comfortable, the tables and booths separate from the bar.

I scan the perimeter, locking my gaze on the corner booth where Mike is sitting. He's speaking to someone, but I can't see whom.

Elbow on the table, he props his head in his hand. He's wearing his favorite low-cut jeans and a ribbed cream sweater I gave him last Christmas.

Always the professional, he keeps his dark hair short around the sides, but it's longer on top, wavy, playful. I remember running my fingers through those locks. They're just as soft as they look.

My tummy flutters with nerves, and, for a moment, I feel transparent, as if he'll see me as desperate. Maybe I am. Maybe I don't care.

I square my shoulders and straighten my blouse. I mash my lips, wishing I'd checked the mirror and added a second coat of lipstick.

But then Mike shifts, and I spot a woman tucked under his arm.

His boss, Noel.

Lip-locked and unashamed as they nuzzle each other's necks.

My heart plummets, along with my misplaced expectations that Mike has changed. Or that he finally wants me after our time apart. By ignoring my numerous texts and calls, his silence pretty much told me we were done. I even sent him a final text explaining that I didn't love him anymore.

So, what game is he playing, texting me? This cat is tired of chasing ghost-mice. But I have to wonder, did he want me to catch him in action? Why the heck am I wasting my energy on him again? If I could, I'd kick my own ass to remind myself why I'm here. It's not a reunion. He's made that clear.

Let go…

Bypassing a woman dressed in western garb, most likely a performer, I stalk toward Mike, my boot lacings binding my straw legs. I wish what I'm seeing is a charade, but it's not. I'm not more than two feet from the cozy duo.

Mike's cheeks are wet, and Noel's kissing away his tears.

Huh? Tears of joy? Sadness? Regret? Loss?

My stomach twists into knots, deepening my queasy feeling of betrayal. The Mike I remember never shed tears, not even when I realized the extent of the accident, not even when I suspected our baby was gone.

The swelling lump in my throat won't deflate,

no matter how many times I gulp air. I don't want to forget the memories we shared. I want to learn from them. It's the pain insisting I show my ex mercy. Not me. "Mike? You texted me. Do you want to talk?"

Mike peels himself from Noel, his puffy, bloodshot eyes the size of quarters, and scrambles out of the booth. "Oh, God, not now."

I pretzel my arms, glaring up at him, scrutinizing his reaction to seeing me. He doesn't seem drunk, and the glass in front of him appears to be iced water with a lemon slice. "Yes. Now. You sent me a text. I thought you wanted to—"

What? Patch up the damage he caused by abandoning me when I needed him most?

Shocker, Emily. He's moved on.

I'm melodramatic, sure, but I feel like he's ripped the bandage off my broken heart all over again when I didn't expect to feel happy to see him. At least happy before I saw Noel. "Say something."

Paling to a sickly green, Mike excuses himself from Noel, who saunters off, clutching her crystal pendant, and seemingly unaffected by my presence.

Good. I don't need a second woman's opinion on what I'm about to say.

Mike threads his fingers through unruly hair,

watching Noel when I need him to look at me. Face me for once. "It should have been me. I wanted us to work out."

He glances in my direction, but his feet don't follow. "I can't do this—I didn't expect—Emily, you shouldn't be…"

"Here? Well, I am. You have something to tell me and this is your chance."

Paling further, he links a string of gibberish, and I feel the need to intercede. In my book, he owes me an explanation of why he abandoned me. "You texted me. I came because I care, but I can see my feelings are as misplaced as ever. Before I leave, tell me this. Did you ever love me? All I wanted was a family, our family, here in Deadwood. Now, I'm wondering if you planned on checking out from the start. Is Noel accepting of how you left me, us?"

"Leave Noel out of this. She's done nothing but help me."

Help you? What about me? "Do you possess the ability to love anyone? Did you ever love me?"

Glancing from side to side, as if unable to meet my gaze, Mike sways and clutches his head. "I'm crazy. You shouldn't be here. You're—"

"Dead pissed that you ignored my texts or calls until today. I called you for weeks. Then you invite me here, only to stage a make-out session with your boss? And tears? Were they real?"

"Yes," he deadpans. "Every emotion I'm feeling is extreme. I miss you. This is where we met, where we fell in love."

"Where we fell out of love and you found your soulmate." I laugh, the sound as bitter and angry as I'm feeling.

"I wish I could change everything. I'm so sorry."

His shocking apology is a slap in the face, even though he meets my stare as if he's telling me the truth. Do I wish to change my past?

He plops into a corner chair and stares up at me, the room's shadows painting his face in ghoulish gray tones. "Emily, I have so much guilt over what happened. Can't you see I'm devastated over losing you? I wanted you. I wanted a family, but then work kept us apart, or I used it as an excuse to avoid my fears of falling in love and then losing you."

But you did. You lost me. You left me alone to grieve. I slide in beside him, stacking my hand on his. I don't know what to say, but when he stiffens at my touch, I realize what we had is gone. No matter if he's sorry or I'm still angry, the candle I once held for him has burned to a threadbare wick. "What now?"

He glances down, staring at our union, however slight. "I was wrong in how I treated you, us. But I'm trying to do what's right. Just know that losing you made me see how important life is instead of working nonstop. I'm not perfect, but I need a fresh start. I'm putting my best self forward from now on."

I don't miss the way he glances at the long-gone trail of Noel. He's made his decision. He's no longer with me. "You're with Noel."

"I don't know how you're here or why I can talk to you so freely, but we both have to be strong. I'm begging you to let me go."

I must, but I sit trembling against the vinyl seat.

He slides a room key onto the table, twirling it in his fingers. "I don't know where you stay, if you need to sleep or rest, but I've found another hotel to stay at. I wish I could give you so much more than an empty room tonight..."

With a final bump, my heart slips, settling in the crevices of my belly, and tears brim on my lashes. I won't give Mike the satisfaction of seeing me cry, but I need a place to stay. If Mike wants me to set him free, who am I to hold him back, forcing him to love me? Forcing myself to love someone who I believe isn't capable of loving me back.

No. I want more, something profound. I want a man who'd swim across a mighty river to be with me.

The lounge spins, and I slide out of the booth, widening my feet for support. I'm on my own. I have been since the accident, and even before. I just didn't realize it until now. Misty memories of the child I thought we'd parent—pushing her on the swing, birthday parties, baby coos, playtime and giggles, our daughter calling me Mom… Those dreams vanish. It's over.

He claims he's changed, but I realize, I don't want to be with a man who traveled too much. Who kept me at a distance. Who worked long hours and overtime. While I don't expect a complete one-eighty in the way I'm feeling, I decide maybe more waits for me if I allow possibilities. The fact is, I don't want to be with a man who doesn't want me. Who might not ever want to be with me. "Face your truth, Mike. It's okay to be with the one person you can't live without, when being with anyone else steals your happiness."

Suddenly, I realize the once heavy scent of cigars and perfume within the lounge seems lighter than ever before.

I take it as a fresh sign I've made the right

choice by confronting Mike. Strangely, the realization that we've split for good no longer grips me with agonizing fear, like I expected. When he stands, I pocket the room key and press a weary smile onto my face. "I won't bother you again. Noel's the one who's always been with you. She's the one you want, and I wish you the best. Good-bye, Mike."

I excuse myself and march toward the elevator. When the doors part, I target the back corner as other hotel guests fill the cube.

On old cables, the elevator chugs upward.

When the elevator doors part, most of the other guests exit left while I pivot right, meandering down to the end of the narrow hallway. No doubt I was the last person holding this feeling of family, and now it's gone, which explains the reason I don't feel as sad over losing Mike as I did from losing my mom and baby.

Tears spill down my hot cheeks regardless. I'm thankful no one can see me as I unlock the door to the honeymoon suite, welcoming the darkness.

I don't need overhead lights to prove the suite's white bedding plumps with goose down or begs me to crawl beneath the sheets. I don't need light to clarify beads of dew on the champagne bottle resting in its frosty container.

I know Mike's expensive tastes, those he now reserves for Noel. But if so, why is the champagne brand my pricey favorite?

"Mike, what are you doing? Why are you holding me here when I need to move on?" I murmur as an excuse to blame someone beside myself for the sadness leaching out of me.

It's over, and we both know that now. But perhaps he asked the concierge to bring up the items as an act of utter truce or as a way to ask for forgiveness. Maybe he planned our doomed reunion all along. Conflicted, I'll never understand him.

Let go….

I slip off my clothes, a small pile forming at my feet. With a tap, I push open the bathroom door, and a cloud of steam billows into the room. Through the dense vapor, I can just make out the sauna tub and a single lit candle burning on a pedestal base. It smells like honey, lavender, and spiced vanilla. Almost edible.

"Really? A bubble bath?"

I pad bare feet across the tiled bathroom floor, careful not to slip as I take off my bracelet, earrings, and ring. The wall guides me toward the light. Until now, I ignored the chill infusing my bones and how that chill amplified over the last hour. But I commit to tossing out my depressed mood, even as water trickles from my eyes and a sob escapes my throat.

Holding onto the edge of the porcelain tub, I enter the bath. Steaming water wraps around me like a hug. "Where is my soulmate? My future? I'm here, waiting on the opposite shore for you. Come to me. Please."

Desperation clings to me. I feel stupid as I sink low into the tub, dunking my head, trying my best to wash off the icky feeling. But as I stretch out my legs, something flesh-like brushes my toes.

I pop up, bursting through the bubbly surface in a panic that sends my heart into overdrive, and water gushes onto the floor.

"Mike, what the hell? Is this a joke? Breaking into my room and staging a romantic interlude after what just went down is a shit move. I don't appreciate—"

"I'm not Mike. He doesn't belong here." The water sloshes, and a stranger holds the candle at his shoulder level.

Momentarily, my voice glues to my throat. I clutch the edge of the tub for dear life. I shut my eyes. *He's not real. He's not here. I'm not noticing his bare skin against my toes.*

I peek, and he's staring right at me with eyes a riveting shade of blue.

Some people run from danger, but, apparently, I don't, not because I can't bolt, but because I'm stone rigid and bare-assed naked. "What do you want? And why are you in my bathtub?"

"You called me here."

His nonchalance troubles me. Did I fall asleep? Pass out? I wiggle my toes against him, noticing a dusting of hairs near his—

I draw up into a fetal ball. I did not just touch his man parts.

"It was my outer thigh. You're safe with me. Promise."

I squint, but the melted candle wax douses the flame, cutting the light in half. "Who are you?"

"You always call me James."

"J-James," I sputter, my lips suddenly trembling along with my body. This isn't right. I'm seeing ghosts. He has to be, except he feels, sounds, and acts alive. "You're a ghost."

"I'm just like you, waiting to be set free."

I cover my face. "This isn't happening."

"But it is, Emily. You must choose… Stay here or let go…"

Along with my fear of my dilemma, another

emotion stirs: hope. I can barely make out James' features through the open sections between my fingers.

Candlelight casts weak shadows across his rugged expression. I shouldn't notice his broad chest, suds cascading over well-developed pecs sprinkled by fine hairs. I shouldn't check out his muscular arms or languish in the timbre of his voice, a sound that wakes desire I've almost forgotten exists.

Most definitely, I shouldn't lean toward him, or allow my leg to shimmy against his, recording the bulk and strength in his thigh.

But more importantly, I refuse to admit my taxed imagination creates a phantom I'm more drawn to than I was ever drawn to Mike or anyone else I dated.

"If you were real, I'd stay… Although you can't be, I wish you were."

"I'm as real as the tears you're crying, and only as far off as your dreams." He swipes his thumb pad across my cheek.

At least I feel him plant his tenderness there a second before his ethereal form vanishes into the rising steam.

CHAPTER 2

James Butler Hickok (JB Hickok, "Wild Bill")

Outside the Bullock Hotel, I press my ass against the brick building and stare up at the lit room where Emily's silhouette passes the draped window a moment before the room's plunged into darkness. One touch, and I've no doubt Emily is the reincarnation of my true love, Agnes. I'd know my wife anywhere, and she, me, dead or alive. But I fear a complication exists as Emily didn't recognize me. Not that hell or high water will stop me from claiming my bride and convincing her to fall in love with me all over again. But is going after her the right thing to do?

Considering I didn't even hold her, kiss her—nor she me—I wonder if I lost my edge. I survived a bear attack, my arm nearly gnawed to pieces. As Marshal, I hunted the lawless. I'm an outlaw in my own right. I killed a few no-good men who lacked common decency and honor. I defended myself with deadly consequences against foes, and I lost a good friend. Since my death on August 2, 1876, I roam Deadwood—over one hundred and fifty years of badass hauntings.

A mortal couple strolls by, while I'm tempted to distract myself from heavy thoughts of Emily by familiarizing myself with the inside of their pockets... One thing a ghost is good for is getting kicks from misplacing people's money in a gambling town and watching their baffled reactions.

I smooth my index finger over my thumb. A single brush of Emily's buttery skin, her wet tear still damp on my pad, and she reduced me to vapor as if she has complete power over my soul.

Contemplating my next move, I slide my hand into my right pocket and fiddle with the locket. Not just any locket. My wife's, who is Emily's great-

great-great-great-grandmother. I didn't have the necklace with me in the sudsy tub, only my birthday suit. But close proximity to the locket ties me to Emily and allows me to find her. To come to her when she calls me.

"Cold night to be holding up a wall with wet hair."

Jane Canary, better known as Calamity Jane, spies me sternly as she strolls up the walk, the overhead awning shadowing her pale features. She's become one of my truest confidants, though in the past, I didn't care for her much. Some claim Jane was my ex-lover, ex-wife, and the mother of a daughter. But that's not true. Agnes, my wife, is now and has always been the one for me.

But Jane's as tough as a mule, stubborn as a nest of wasps, and more like me than I care to admit, which is why we're friends in the afterlife. "Didn't have time to blow-dry."

On the breezy night, the ruffles at the base of her skirt flutter. "Since when are you going all girly?"

I roll the ends of my mustache. Facts be facts, I watch Jane's back, and she's still watching mine. We're nearly as connected at the hip—or the casket—as I am to Emily. Jane ensures we'll remain close by taking up space in the Mt. Moriah Cemetery right next to where my body lies buried, nestled between hers and prospector Potato Creek Johnny.

But there are things I can't tell neither Jane nor Emily about me. Secrets I keep—one being the locket, which I snatched the day of the accident. The other even more incriminating.

If Jane finds out I'm keeping something from her, she's liable to kick my ass into a fifth dimension. I can't risk losing Emily now. "Something happened."

Mimicking my pose, Jane parks herself beside me, massaging something small in the palm of her hand. "I can tell by the way you're fiddlin' with your 'stache, it's something big. But I know you, JB. You're gonna spill the goods to me eventually. Might as well pull off the scab while I have time to tend your wound."

Yeah, Jane knows me. But Emily doesn't. If she discovers from Jane that I stole her family heirloom as a way to track her, she's smart enough to follow the breadcrumbs and uncover the truth behind the cause of the accident, which led to her death. I can't allow anyone else to do my job of consoling her from that shock.

Worse, all of Agnes' past lives will reveal

themselves to Emily. She'll see my twisted motives as a way to satisfy my selfish desires to keep her locked to Deadwood. Poor Emily still believes she has a mortal future. That she's physically alive. She's not ready to learn the truth that she died, or that her hopes and dreams of some human future will never come true. If she learns the truth, she'll never fall for me.

I pull out my pocket watch, noting the new day. "Time. I need more time," I mumble.

"For what? You're starting to scare me." Jane stands on tiptoes, examining my expression and checking me for madness.

In the shadows, a figure darts across Main Street and disappears into thin air as a wicked screech that could be owl or spirit echoes above, the sound giving me shivers, similar to the flag waving high above Bullock's.

Maybe I'm here to prepare Emily for the truth of her fate. Not to fall in love.

No. I sweep that thought away. No rush exists, now that she's here with me. I hurt Agnes by dying five months after our wedding day, after I promised we'd build a happy home together. Hurting her will kill me all over again, and I can't bear for any soul to wind up like me and Jane, searching for clues leading to an afterlife of peace that may or not exist. I won't tolerate witnessing another pissed-off, restless soul, who realizes everyone they ever loved has moved on and they're left behind. No, sir.

Jane jabs me in the side with her elbow, snapping me out of my reverie.

"What's going on?"

I withdraw my hand, instead folding my palms over my twin ivory-handled revolvers, taking my time before I answer. "I must convince someone to fall in love with me. Once she does, I can help her see the truth that she's living among spirits. Plenty to be had in Deadwood. Is that Old-Tyme Hoedown still happening behind the Bullock Hotel?"

Cocking her head, Jane scrutinizes me hard. "You mean a dance?"

"Yeah, a dance. Ladies and gentlemen. Where people fall in love. Surely, a memory will jar this spirit's recollection of the man she once promised to love forever."

Jane raises a brow and flips her hair back over her shoulders, looking exasperated, but I don't blame her. I grow tired of my machinations, too.

She covers her chest with her hand. "A dance doesn't make a woman fall in love with a man. It's him showing her his vulnerable side. She has to trust you to fall for you. You can't fool her into liking you."

The night air temp drops, or maybe it is the truth of Jane's words hitting home. I'll need to open up to Emily, slicing old wounds and letting them bleed out, something I naturally resist. Especially when the last thing I want is to hurt her.

Crap. I blow out a nice fat ring of mist that distorts as soon as it hits the chilled air. "I don't need to impress anyone or puke old regrets," I insist as I jab a finger at my chest to make a point. "It's me. Wild Bill. What's not to love?"

Jane waves a hand, clearly not buying what I'm selling.

She peers closer. "There's something going on behind those sapphire irises. You're holding back. You want her to fall for you, you gotta gouge out those eyes and let her see the man behind the walled-up façade."

I flutter my lashes mockingly, knowing damn well she's right.

"But I think you have a shot," she adds.

Checking out Jane's sure gaze, I lean in. "How can you tell?"

"I haven't seen a spark in your eyes since 1876, when you returned to Deadwood married to Agnes.

JB, tell me you're not meddling. This town took forever to recover from the Great Deadwood Fire of 1879."

Meddling schmeddling. "Town needed a clean sweep. Besides, I was pissed. I may have won that card game, if it wasn't for Jack McCall losing his shit and taking out his life's problems on me. I would have returned to my wife! So, yes. Meddling is exactly what I did when I spotted Agnes three months ago and she collided with me, and I her. Then yesterday, Agnes showed up here in town. In my bathtub, while I was in it. Naked as a day-old eagle."

"Wait. Agnes is here?"

A gunshot rings out, sizzling past my left ear, and we both duck as we slide around the corner. Damn outlaws, still shooting up the town. I reach out, pulling Jane within whisper distance. "Yes, Agnes is here. Emily is the reincarnation of Agnes, her distant granddaughter."

Jane slaps her knee. "Well that explains the woman I crossed paths with at the Bullock Hotel. Damn woman gave me the shakes. She's the spitting image of Agnes, now that you're telling me she's here. But you can't make contact with this Emily if she doesn't know she's dead. Something disastrous could happen."

I kick at a clump of sawdust that's been tracked out of Seth's Cellar, I suspect. I need to make a choice to pursue Emily, and I'm torn. What if I screw up and lose her forever? "Agnes—Emily, saw me first three months ago. We crashed, literally. Something disastrous happened."

I hold up a hand to stop Jane's incoming homily.

"Give me a minute." I ponder a moment, gathering the memory of the accident and weeding through what I *can* share. "Emily believes she's still alive. I can't sit around idle while she resists fate, but I don't want to let her go, either. Not after I promised Agnes and she promised me we'd be together for an eternity, no matter fire and brimstone."

Jane clutches her chest and shakes her head, her fine hair floating about her shoulders. "Lord have mercy. This is worse than I expected. You can't control another's fate."

I shove from the wall to face Jane. "That's BS and you know it. If Emily and I weren't supposed to meet again, then why did we? I'm here for a reason. She's my reason."

"You can't stop fate, JB, not even your own. You also can't go blurting to this poor woman she's a damn ghost. She could go mad, like William

Emery Adams. She would disappear. If she does, should you go after her, both of your souls may be lost forever. Please tell me you're not risking souls?"

"Could. Would. Should. Every direction is an unknown variable. But you know me, Jane. I'm not a man who understands how to back down once I'm confronted with a challenge, especially to reclaim my wife. I only hope I don't regret what I'm about to do."

She darts out her hand, gripping my arm. "Damn it, Bill. You're hung up on this woman, and have been since she captured your attention walking a tightrope. It's the danger you're hungry for. The taboo. Adventure. Even I let go of you. I'm still here. For the most part, happy, but I consider the reason I'm stuck in limbo is to help you move on and realize you lived *your* life to the fullest. Forget Agnes. Forget Emily, me, all of us. Forgive yourself for the wrongs you're blaming yourself for and set yourself free."

For once, I don't want Jane pointing out my faults or wedging herself between my goals of reuniting with my wife. "I can't allow anyone to risk their soul to save mine, and I can't forget those I wronged. You know me. I don't deserve to move on because I don't deserve forgiveness. Plain and simple. So I choose to keep Emily here."

"Stop believing lies. You have a kind heart. You're a good man. People love you. You *both* deserve to be freed from this place of limbo."

I chuckle. "I'm not liked by everyone. We both know it. Until I convince Emily to fall in love with me, I'm not leaving this place. When I'm ready, I'll reconnect with her, show her a good time, the truth, yada, yada, and hope she accepts me and decides to stay. Then my true love and I will be together forever. Here in Deadwood."

"This isn't about when *you're* ready. Or her staying in Deadwood. It's about Emily. The longer she remains as a spirit here, the harder it will be for her to leave. You can't hold her to this veil. You have to be smart about this. You can't go after her. She has to summon you, which I assume she did last night, organically, as you keep glancing up at the room I see she's taken over as her own. She doesn't even realize who she is, from what I can tell. Or *what* she is: dead. What do you plan on doing about jogging her memories that won't have her freaked?"

I dip my hand into my left pocket, rolling a specific cellular device in my palm. I poured out my soul to her yesterday, pretending to be Mike, leading the two to sever their connection. I even went as far as haunting Mike and Noel's room, forcing them to go somewhere else. I'm an outlaw, after all. One who loves hard. "Oh, I plan on kick-starting Emily's memories any damn way I can."

"Don't do anything reckless. Promise me."

A growl percolates up my throat at the memory of the car accident—and my involvement. "Emily called for me last night. Twice. Once when she was with Mike. Another in the tub. She summoned me, and I won't deny her."

"Wait. What? Are you saying you tracked this woman for a quarter of a year and are just now getting around to interacting with her? That's not like you to wait."

Truth is, I don't want to screw this up. "No. Emily appeared yesterday of her own doing. I believe it's because her ex laid her ashes to rest at Mt. Moriah."

I omit the part about stealing Mike's cell phone the day of the accident, lurking as Emily sent text after text and call after call, before I decided to intercept as her one and only true love. "Then last night, she reached out to me, like I said," I defend pointlessly, as Jane rolls her eyes.

Anyhow... "As I was saying, a few months ago, near Mt. Moriah Cemetery, Emily saw me. The car she was riding in drove right through me, and our souls slammed into each other. It was my wife, Jane. She recognized me one hundred times over, but then I felt her panic, her fear, as her human life faded after her car was struck by a second car that came out of nowhere. Regret traps me to this world, and I'm tired. Can't you see how badly I want to hold her again, love her?"

Jane's discerning gaze doesn't surprise me. We both know if I scare Emily, she's as good as gone. If I force our connection, I could initiate a domino effect of past lives resurfacing, and her reliving each one, which is sure to scare her into the abyss. I could lose her when I just found her.

Jane motions toward Saloon No. 10. "So what's your plan?"

Glancing behind me and satisfied I'm not being trailed, I join her. "Not sure, except I won't risk losing Emily. I'm holding tight until we're both flying off into the light."

"The light?"

Jane's high-pitched alarm shakes me. "Yes, ascension. Whatever."

"For all you know, Emily could be like me, trapped without a clue, except for the desire to collect these damn keys." Jane digs into her skirt pocket and comes up with a lint ball and a handful of antique, mismatched, tarnished keys.

Objects and purpose tie spirits to the human world. Jane insists she has an undeniable urge to find a particular match to the damaged key she wears hanging from a leather strap tied around her neck. She deduced the key leads to unclaimed riches hidden inside the Levinson Block buildings, which housed Levinson's jewelry store in 1909. Now, the building serves patrons of the relocated Saloon No. 10, and the Deadwood Social Club. I contemplate my true purpose as a thought strikes me. "You think Emily returned to Deadwood looking for something besides me?"

"Yes and no. You may be her harbinger and guide, but I believe, like all of us, she's looking to find herself."

Wholeheartedly, I believe this to be true. Only, what if Emily learns the truth of who she really is and realizes, after one hundred and fifty years and several lifetimes of experiences, she's changed her mind about loving me? Changed her mind about sharing an eternal bond and fading into the sunset together?

No. I shake the vision.

As if Jane reads my mind, she nudges me. "Fate's in control. Agnes might disappear for a while, but she'll come back in one form or another.

You'll catch another chance to connect with her, if it's meant to be."

I shake my head, knocking my hat to the ground and dusting up the crown. What if Jane's wrong? What if saving her boyfriend, Mike Williams, my second chance to save my reincarnated pard, was what I needed to do to move on, but I'm too big a fool to pry open my damaged eyes and see the light?

Try as I may, I can't brush away the shame I carry for distracting Emily in the first place, which led to the car accident. If sweet Emily finds out what I did, she'll hate me. I'll be doomed to walk the earth for an eternity, loveless, lonely, a lost soul.

Forget that I rescued this Mike from the wreckage, who dragged Emily from the mangled steel carriage and held her until help arrived. Not that help did her much good. Saving one human isn't enough. "Emily is my wife. I'm her husband. I'd expect her to tackle and hogtie me, if my soul is at risk. To free her from limbo, I'll do whatever it takes, even if I have to seduce her all over again and it takes a million years."

I punctuate my promise, stomping my custom boots and righting my hat.

"Part of me wants to warn you to stay away from her, the other wants to help you."

I pause, gathering my mental bearings, just as the sun makes its first appearance. "Not this time, Jane. What I'm doing, I'm doing alone."

She holds up keys to the sunlight, the morning rays diving through the decorative handles and stamping her cheek with Celtic patterns. "Her antique store is a nice place to find keys. I'll see you around, JB. Or not."

As Jane saunters off, I spot Mike on a mission, heading for the Bullock Hotel. Technically, after laying Emily's ashes to rest yesterday, he shouldn't have the ability to interact with her, so maybe he has unfinished business with the hotel…

Still, I actually feel sorry for the unfortunate, suffering soul. Resisting the pull to this woman is as frugal as preventing a boulder from rolling downhill after it's ass over end and spiraling out of control. Momentum keeps me rolling, gaining speed, as well. I won't give up until I make Emily mine. Consequences be damned.

Besides, I'm a patient man, as history proves. I waited a near decade, love letters our only means of communication way back when, before opportunity presented itself, and I made Agnes my wife.

As a ghost, I have all the time in the world. And I'll wait for Emily to call on me. She will with a nudge. I'm certain of that.

So, I do the one thing necessary. My first step. I raise the locket and press a kiss to the washed-out gold inscription on the back.

CHAPTER 3

Emily

My chest suddenly tingles where my locket once laid, and visions of last night's bathtub man stalk my thoughts. Who was the man who joined me briefly in the bath last night? He looked so familiar, but his foggy features seem as trapped as if held behind opaque glass.

Counting the change in my register drawer distracts me for only a moment. I shouldn't devote time to an apparition of my own making, yet I can't get him out of my mind. The way he ran a calloused thumb across my cheek, the sureness of his calm, reassuring voice, the dreams I had of him later that night as I drifted off to sleep. We were hand in hand, and when he brought his lips against mine, butterflies in flight pirouetted inside of me and a full orchestra delightfully played. I giggle out loud at my dramatics. I'm still feeling the sensation of tiny wings beating against the walls of my belly. Unsurprisingly, a deep need to know him rises with every tick of the clock.

Which reminds me. Wild Bill Days is already in motion, as outside tourists practically stampede down Main Street.

I shake my head as I make my way to the door, switching the Deadwood Antiques sign from closed to open. Today could be my lucky day. It's Saturday, and the sound of an acoustic guitar filters into the shop. Under each awning, trinket stands, flags, and memorabilia proudly display the town's lively frontier. I check the cash register once again, counting the bills when, behind me, the doorbell chimes.

"Ma'am."

Ma'am. I'm twenty-five, hardly more than a Miss. But, I admit, stress aged me. Fine lines appear at the corners of my eyes, my skin holds a paler appearance, and my chestnut-colored hair no longer weaves with lustrous golden tones according to my reflection in glass case. On the contrary, Miss no longer fits my womanly curves, my state of dress, nor the state of my seasoned mind.

"I like your hair falling loose about your shoulders."

The baritone tugs me around along with the personal statement. I pinch my eyes as the vision from last night becomes corporeal. Only, I must be imagining things. I almost ask if I know him, and if he was in the bath with me. "Thank you, sir."

"Sir?" He chuckles. "Folks around here call me JB."

JB. Saying his name in my head earns a second glance. If the cowboy was anywhere but Deadwood, his looks could pass as refined, but he holds a fearless gaze that coaxes my full attention. Dirty-blond hair peeks from under his black cowboy hat, which rides low across his forehead. His theatrical style of dress suggests he's an entertainer, but, more so, a faint image of his silhouette appears at the back of my mind. *James.*

I must confess, a nervous energy stretches my skin to near bursting. I check myself in the full-length mirror near the register. Blue jeans, check. Buttoned-down red blouse, one half of my shirt tucked into the front of my pants to add a hint of fashion sense, I think. Gold hoops that match my bracelet and ring, which only accentuate the missing necklace.

I button up my shirt another notch. I don't want to be reminded of what I lost. "JB. I'm Emily. I heard a lot about you."

"Says everyone, but they don't know me like you did once upon a time."

Know him? I tap my forehead, frustrated that my mind seems to unlock some doors to my memories but keeps others shut. Did we date? Maybe when I was in high school? Were we *involved?* I'd remember, right?

I shiver, but I don't think he notices.

He pivots slowly, adding a high-pitched whistle, as if he's impressed with the store, and I flush at his appreciation of the past.

"Nice shop you have, but I have a better place we should check out."

His slight southern drawl begs my uninterrupted attention as I mull over his suggestion. Where is he from? Here? Next, did I hear him right? Is he asking me out? Should I risk going with him, risk putting myself out there? Should I risk finding out if true love exists? Eternal love?

Not a chance. At least my mind insists I keep to my resolve. Nervously, I busy my hands at the counter, while the cowboy's handsome looks melt my insides. I blame my sensual reaction on last night's vision, the stranger's touch, his gentleness. This man is the spitting image of my dream man. Or is he? Could he be more than who my mind conjures?

He rests an elbow on the counter, leaning in. "You're even more beautiful than I recall, and I swear I remember every microscopic detail about you."

My cheeks burn, and, no matter how I try, I can't corral my focus as he bores his cobalt gaze into mine. His expression hints at an intimacy I wish I remembered. "Where did we meet?"

He shuffles his boots, butting the tips against the counter's base. "Here, there, and all the places in between."

Ah, a poet *and* an entertainer. Over six feet tall, with an impressive stature, I stare, hoping to pry out some bit of shared history. A flash of familiarity glints through my mind, and I chase after it as it fades. I definitely recall him from before. "Seriously, who are you to me?"

He glances down at his boots, shaking his head, and I feel his disappointment.

"I can show you once we get out of this shop. It's depressing, dark, and dulls your pretty blue eyes."

Sensing his eagerness to leave, I brush on a smile, hoping to dampen the heat rising to my cheeks. It's been a long time since I received a compliment. My mother used to say wearing a smile is like bluffing in a game of cards. From experience, replacing a sappy mood or an uncomfortable situation with a smile fooled me into believing I had a fabulous day. Wanting just that, I plaster a smile on my face. "Thank you for the compliment, but, if the shop's so bad, why are you here?"

"Wouldn't want to be anywhere else, at the moment." He tips his hat, pushing sturdy arms across the glass until he fully rests on his elbows, peering up at me with a haunting, inescapable presence.

This must be what the doctors describe as missed time or moments of amnesia. Time skips following the accident, like the pause between waves. A full two seconds tick by until I squirm with puzzling discomfort. Then, I vaguely recognize the quirk in his cheek, denting with promises of a misplaced wit, and a fine scar riding his thick brow—same as the man in my tub.

It hits me as I recall that during Wild Bill Days nearly a decade ago, I once posed as one of the swanky saloon girls before I went off to college. "Are you a member of the Main Street Shootouts historic street show?"

He fumbles with his hat, pinching at the brim, and an amused guffaw rumbles up his throat.

He sounds almost offended. Is he a potential buyer of the shop? I expect sooner or later the advertisement posted in the Black Hills Pioneer will attract a buyer. At the thought, my tummy flops, but not in a pleasurable way. What will I do without the store? My time? Will I be forced to move on before I'm really ready to let go?

"Tell me something. What's a beautiful woman like you waiting for when you should be out strolling the sunny streets, soaking up a tan, while I escort you around town?"

Oh, the theatrics. Well, this is Deadwood. No telling what kind of mischief preceded the cowboy's visit. I close my jaw, realizing he's shocked me.

Similarly, Mike surprised me, practically telling

me when and where we'd date. He decided we were an item at the second meeting. Once engaged, he orchestrated the secret trip to Deadwood, which led to the accident.

I shiver and hug my arms. *Don't think about him.*

"I could replace that frown with a very satisfied smile, if you give me a chance."

JB, or whatever his real name is, lifts the corner of his mouth, waiting for a response from me, as he holds out his hand.

The cowboy isn't Mike. He's not some bathtub phantom. He's just a man looking for a little fun from a woman who wants to live. In truth, if I want to settle in Deadwood and have a family, I must let down my guard and begin somewhere. Do I dare take his offer? Am I ready to go?

I glance at my pale arms, realizing JB knows me. Perhaps he can jar a memory or two, help me remember where I lost my locket. Maybe he can initiate something even better than I imagined. Better than whispers of the past.

The door chimes again, shocking me out of my fantasy.

Two customers enter the shop, a full band of sunlight spearing the dim space, little dust particles floating all about the room.

"You can see I'm busy, so unless you can miraculously produce my missing locket, I'll take a raincheck." I pull out one drawer, searching the space, then another while making mental excuses. I can't run off with a stranger, not with my responsibilities tying me here. Even if I want to.

I spot myself in the mirror, and then catch him staring at me with those gorgeous blue eyes, speckles of gray and black emphasizing the dangerous depths. "I could use a little sunshine, and I appreciate the offer, but I have to watch the store."

"I'll wait." He tepees his fingers, seeming to look straight through me, challenging me with his gaze to close up shop now.

As spark turns to flames, taking purchase inside my chest, I warn myself not to rush in as I did with Mike. Not to put the cart before the horse, as they say. "That won't be necessary. I'm sure you have more important things to occupy your time. Rehearsing for the part of Wild Bill. You're the lead of the shootout scene, right?"

He groans and raises a hand to his chin.

I can't tell if he's pleased or irritated, but I'm curious about him.

"You mean, am I an actor who's trying to pull

off pretending to be myself? No. I'm the real thing. I'm staying right here until I get my way. With you. Take a chance on me, Emily. I promise to show you the time of your life, and you can be my leading lady."

By the glint in his narrowed gaze, he's crazy serious, and now I'm scared of the possibility. I'm not ready. I don't consider myself rude, so I don't call out his declaration to be the end-all to my problems. He's not the real Wild Bill Hickok any more than I'm the real Agnus Mersman Thatcher Lake Hickok, which would make me his wife. Otherwise, I'd be dead, or seeing ghosts, or insane.

God, what if I'm the one who's gone crazy?

I pinch my arm and flinch from the twinge of pain. No. I'm one hundred percent present. "Excuse me for a moment, will you?"

JB blocks my path a beat before allowing me to pass, but that's when I brush against his arm with mine.

A flash of lightning rips through us, the lingering static gripping me and freezing both of our feet to the wood-planked floor and to each other. Locked together, we both gasp. His familiarity drills into me, unlocking a memory that's filled with the heat of a thousand blistering suns. He ghosts his mouth over mine, and his mustache dusts my lips. He spears my mouth with his tongue, and he undoubtedly claims my body with eager hands that I encourage with pleasurable moans.

I'm yours.

You're mine.

Forever…

Echoes of long-ago promises rip through my mind. My spaghetti legs fail to hold me, but JB's right here, supporting me, erasing my loneliness and panic. I instantly know JB is not what I call him, and the bathtub scenario isn't our first time neck-deep in black water. "James? What's happening?"

He staggers back a step, severing our connection, and winded. "Agnes? Darling, is it you?"

Agnes? Unsure what's happened, I jerk clear, slicing the jolting connection even more. But I don't forget the kiss, the hunger in him, the desire still welling inside of me. Or my name. *Agnes.* She belonged to James Hickok. She was his wife. My distant grandmother. But I belong to James now, and he to me, as if Agnes and I are inseparable. But when? How?

Reincarnation.

I shake my head, snapping free of the memory

of James at the accident. Clearly, Mike interacted with James, who pulled Mike from the wreckage. "Excuse me. Customers need my help."

Okay, they don't, but I'm shocked, and my mind struggles to make sense of what happened, what's happening. To buy myself time, I hustle toward the duo, but James is a breath away, hot on my heels.

How can he be *the* James Hickok? My ancestor's husband. Simultaneously, I can't help but see everything around me as a sign, the old meshing with the new, or the reverse, as if I'm caught in some kind of Wild West time warp.

Even the couple drifting down the aisle has an uncanny familial resemblance, and their attire matches a period of time that isn't of today.

They hold up, and the woman raises a framed photo. An adoring grin paints their faces.

I know the picture well. It's of Agnes and James Hickok in Cheyenne on their wedding day, March 5th, 1876. Could it be a version of them, trapped in time, here in Deadwood? Still together and in love? Happy?

"You'll never have what you want if you don't let go. Come with me. Please."

At James' request, I pinch my eyes as his plea

vibrates down my spine. The outlaw I heard of is not a man who pleads for anything, according to historical facts.

He takes. He stakes. He claims.

What would it be like if this man swam across a river for me? Or I to him?

I can't discount that James left out an essential part of his request. What would he get out of flirting with me and coaxing me on a date? Why is he so concerned about me when my memory of him scatters like tumbleweeds in a storm? Does he believe I'm Agnes? Do I?

I called for a lover last night in the tub. I thought of him the moment before he walked into the shop. Is he real?

Deadwood hauntings...

"Come with me." He stretches out his hand, which edges into my peripherals.

I remind myself history proves true love is doomed, no matter how badly couples covet eternal love. Fate destroyed my parents' love, mine and Mike's, and, most cruelly, my ancestor Agnes' new marriage when Jack McCall murdered James.

What if Fate presents us with a second chance?

I glance around the store, at the dust and useless things. If I don't take a chance now, I may never get another opportunity. And hey, if this is nothing more than a rebound and I really am crazy, there are worse people I could get over Mike with.

He motions for me, curling fingers in my view, and tempting me to take up his proposal.

"Trust me, Emily."

If I don't let go of my past, I could miss the opportunity to explore a new way of life and love.

I pivot to face him, and the look in his glistening eyes steals my breath. His smile covets my soul. "I'm scared," I admit.

Bending over me, he touches his forehead to mine, and I breathe him in.

"Me too. But I can teach you what love feels like, and, if I'm lucky, maybe you can teach me a thing or two."

It's the strangest sensation, but I feel warm, safe, and treasured. I feel protected. I feel claimed. True love doesn't exist, I once thought. But what if I'm wrong? Don't we all want to be wrong about that?

I do. So, I slide my hand into his, and he clutches me as if he'll never let go, pulling me through the open door, toward second chances, and into the light.

CHAPTER 4

James

The sunny day shadows Emily's presence tenfold. Never in my life have I been as all-absorbed with a woman as I am right now. But as I check Emily, I consider her low mood. She's just broken up with her ex, who, no doubt, reminds her of the child she's lost—of all she's lost. Could she want to escape her life? "Would you consider pretending to be Agnus today? Just one day, dress up, play the part of your true ancestor?"

She drops my hand, and I bite bullets, thinking I offended her, but then she adds a little skip in her step.

She glances up at me, a smile pulling at her lips. "You know Agnes was such an exciting woman. I always wished I could be her. In fact, I can't imagine what it would be like to be her for a day. Dress up in period clothing like you, or maybe adorn tights and walk the wire, ride an elephant and appease crowds. Or just hang with you and see where that leads. So, yes, I would like that very much. Only, because our shop doesn't sell period clothes or jewelry, I'm not sure where to buy my outfit for today, and I'm really missing my locket I lost in the accident."

The locket. I fight against telling her I have it, which could blow up my plans. Instead, I take her hand and lead her toward the sounds of pumping music at the end of Main Street, trying my darnedest to push a sappy smile onto my face. I almost consider stooping a bit, since I tower over most of the townsfolk. If Jane spots me, I can't risk her making a scene. But hell, Emily is my wife. I have every right to show her off as long as she's with me.

Through the throng of tourists and spirits, we zigzag, making our way to the shop. After five minutes, we dart into Woody's Wild West Photography, a boutique where mortals can dress up and have their pictures taken. The outfits range from feathers to leathers and every sort of fabric in between. But I spot a pair of nickel-plated pistols in the case that resemble the ones parked in my holster. "Ready to have some fun?"

While I appreciate my guns' details as compared to the plastic counterfeits, Emily glances around the store, costumes hanging from hooks that once held the real thing.

"Now I know where everyone shops for period clothing. How about this gown. I love deep-purple, which nearly matches the color of your eyes."

My heart puddles at my feet, she's so damn adorable, noticing things about me I forgot the same way Agnes used to. The dress is floor length and bustled at the back. Buttons start at the bosom and descend below the waist, which is slim and will accentuate her tiny waist made even smaller by the corset. A bow covers the bustle in the back. Ruffles skirt the attached waistcoat, bottom of the dress, and sleeves. A cream-colored undergarment teases my memory of Agnes, stripped down to nothing but thin linen and lace. "It's perfect. Try it on. We have some serious dancing to do tonight."

She clutches the dress, and then pauses, checking the tag dangling from the sleeve. "I best not. It's expensive."

I dig into my pockets, cupping the generous sampling of crisp bills. Noting the roll is beginning to make my cock look like it has a twin, I slap the wad onto the counter. "Band's waiting for its newest dancer."

She squeals and darts into the dressing room.

I run my hand along the counter, snagging back the roll. One hundred, two hundred, three, four... I shove the amount over the edge of the counter. I may be an outlaw, breaking into the store while the owner is closed, but I'm one to take care of the living in this town. Mrs. Sally Bennet, owner of the store, lost her husband last year. She could use the cash. The rest I pocket for later.

"James, what do you think? I mean, it's beautiful, but my...my boobs are ready to escape, and I don't think this corset will allow me to eat."

My jaw drops, and I'm not sure if I can close it. Agnes. My beautiful wife. I brush my damp eyes. Must be dust in the air...

"Say something. You don't like it?"

When I can work my throat past the budding ache, I pull her against me and kiss her like it's both the first and last time. She opens for me and I dive in, jousting, teasing, and claiming her mouth in a savage kiss filled with raw lust, eternal love, and fathomless adoration. "I missed you…" I breathe against her lips just as the air fills with static, locking us together in a blinding memory once again.

The circus crowds that fill the tent punch to their feet, adding a deafening applause. From the first moment I spot Agnes Thatcher Lake, the tightrope walker, the acrobat, the horse rider and lion tamer, adorned in her flesh-toned tights and glitter, I'm paralyzed by her grace and beauty.

But then she's airborne, and I'm gaping, perched on my seat and ready to spring onto the dusty arena, ready to catch her. Static rips through me, and she locks her gaze on mine.

I almost scramble back out of my seat, and our connection sparks an instant before it turns to blistering embers. Then she's flying through the air, reaching for the bar that's swinging her way, clutching the handle at the very instant before it pendulums the opposite direction, while my heart fuses to hers.

I know, the moment we connect, she's mine though I never met her.

Like a boomerang, the vision flies off only to return with the reality of who I'm holding. Emily. Uncomfortable with sharing my vulnerabilities, I ease her back, attempting to catch my breath and my control. "Are you okay?"

She clutches her head, massaging her temples. "I don't know. It's weird and has to have something to do with my accident. Every time I kiss you, I get these flashbacks that I don't think are mine, or they're dreamlike. Maybe of me and my ex, but I'm not sure. Did you see and feel the vision too?"

"No," I blurt, escaping the fact our shared visions are as real for me as they are for her. "I only hear the music out on the street."

While she's regaining her balance, I roll the corners of my mustache, chastising my damn self for continuing to lie to her. That fact brings me around, though. If it wasn't for me, she'd be here enjoying her family, her daughter, for God's sake. So, I must consider what she'd be enjoying if I hadn't sentenced her here.

"You know, you always fuss with your mustache when you're overthinking. What are you worried about?"

I take her head in my hands and kiss the top of it. "How you rescue me every day. Don't forget that."

Out on the street, everyone is checking out the queen on my arm. Yeah, I'm soaking it in, feeling like a king without limits. "Let's say you can do anything you want. What would you do?"

She glances up at me, and I see a bit of hesitation cross her expression as she taps her cheek.

"Well, first, I'd get up on stage with the star of the Main Street show and become one of Reba's backup singers. After the show, I'd dance until my feet hurt so badly I earn blisters and a hot bath. And a burger. I'd want a big, juicy beef burger with all the trimmings."

I chuckle out loud. Sure as shit, this is my wife. I squeeze her hand, noticing her grip is less tacky than it was the first time I touched her, but that raw buzz hasn't let up. Can Emily sense destiny has locked us firmly together? "What else?"

"What else? I just want to be someone else for a while. You mastered it, so show me what to do."

I lengthen my stride just a bit and offer her my arm, which she takes, linking us together. "It's easy. Act natural."

She giggles, her laughter like sunshine and warming me through and through.

"People are staring."

I raise her dainty hand to my lips and almost groan. I'm hers, and I'm about to show off the grand prize. "Let them do their worst."

"Agnes. Bill." A couple pass, adding a curt nod.

Emily leans in. "The woman's brooch is beautiful, and I adore her striped skirt. The man wears a sheriff badge, but I can't put a name to the faces they're portraying. Who are they?"

She should be asking *what*; they're ghosts who don't know they're dead, like her. For a moment, I consider whether showing her the ghosts of Deadwood is the best way to introduce her to the truth. Is there a better way? "Friends. Sheriff Seth Bullock and his wife, Martha."

"Part of the show. Of course. I spot the remarkable resemblance now. The chamber of commerce and those running the Wild Bill Days think of everything, even down to the mud seeping up through the bricks."

I hitch my arm around her waist, hiking her over a puddle from last night's storm. Like me, apparently, she sees both the muck at her feet as well as the brick-lined road, two moments in time overlapping. Does she wonder about the others strolling past, crisscrossing the street, ducking into local establishments, mothers with their children, and gunslingers looking for trouble? Some folks who may have died in the 1879 fire I caused in a fit of rage from not being able to return to walk among the living? For not being able to claim my wife?

Some who perished as the result of a smallpox epidemic, a near ten days after I was killed? "Yes, the performers are quite realistic. But you steal the show, Pet."

She shakes her head, her dark hair floating about her shoulders. "I think my mother mentioned James had a nickname for his wife. You really dial into your character. Mom also mentioned the Bullocks during her historical presentations, as well as some of the other people strolling the town. Some sure look familiar."

I'm an honest man, so continuing to royally fib nearly doubles me over. "Remember, performing is having the ability to convince the audience you're the real thing."

Another ghost sashays toward us again. Madam Dufran is a spirit stuck here, disbelieving she's dead or, like me, unworthy of moving on. I ponder, as I take in the misty apparitions that haunt the town, if they're all dead because of me, linked somehow, or simply an illusion.

"Agnes, your dress is stunning. But I'm certain it would shine with a parure, or, at a minimum, a pendant to go with your décolletage bodice."

The only thing Emily needs to shine is me locked at her side for eternity.

Emily tips her head. "Thank you, yes, we're headed to the jewelers now."

I tip my hat to the woman who once was the owner of the most profitable brothel in Deadwood, all the while hoping she doesn't stir my anxiety further. "Madam DuFran."

Madam Dora Dufran folds one hand over the other, white gloves disappearing under her sleeves. "This must be your wife, Agnes. You are exquisite, my dear. I would have hired you in a heartbeat. But now I know why Bill never drops by my establishment."

Emily pauses, bending at the waist and adding a little bow. "Thank you, and your outfit is lovely, as well. What establishment are you speaking of."

"Tripple Ds, of course."

Emily glances up at me, and I can see her wheels spinning. *Who is this woman? What is Tripple Ds? Why don't you stop by her store?*

"Tripple Ds stands for Dining, Drinking, and Dancing."

"Among other things." Dora spreads a seductive look across her face as she fiddles with her brooch.

Emily must catch on, because she squeezes my arm. "Madam—"

"Call me Dora."

"Dora, it's been so nice meeting you, but we must be on our way. We have a full day ahead of us, and I need to purchase jewelry. Enjoy your day."

"You really should come by. We welcome couples…"

As Dora continues in the opposite direction, I hitch Emily's arm in mine. "You're doing great. But stay away from her. She has a cat fetish, among other things."

Emily laughs, a hearty sound, bubbling with amusement. "I had a feeling what she was selling had to do with pussy."

Instinct takes over, and I drag her into the alley between the two buildings, crushing my lips against her naughty mouth.

The swing beside Emily sways empty. She's elementary age, wearing a dress that reveals her boney legs. It must be fall because burgundy and mustard-colored leaves flutter down from the young sycamore tree… It's as if I'm there with her but then as if she's showing me a snapshot in time.

The tree's trunk doubled in size, and I'm in her head, eavesdropping on her lingering thought as she's making out with a boy. "The bark isn't as rough as I expected against my back, kissing Carl for the first time…"

Spring growth weighs down the tree's limbs made lush

with green leaves. Emily's cheeks glisten with tears and her red eyes can't hide her pain. I read the initials carved in the cambium: Tate & Carl.

Winter is harsh in South Dakota. The tree's sturdiness acts as a pillar, straining to hold up snow-covered skeletal limbs. Emily struggles, alone, to refasten the weathered rope swing. She's maybe college age, a bit younger than she is now. I want to help her wrap the limb with rope, to balance the wooden seat. I want to push her and hold her while she sobs.

Snow puddles, leaving soggy earth. Nothing remains but char and splintered wood of the tree. As far as I can tell, it's been struck by lightning. When I approach Emily, she's slumped against the trunk, talking to the tree. "I made the decision to keep the baby…"

All but a stump remains, but it must be early spring of the same year. Once again, she converses with what's left of the tree. "The nurse came in and told me I'm having a girl. I was so excited. I called Mike, but he didn't pick up. After two texts and the third time trying on the phone, I left a message…"

I'm in the tub when she enters, pulling off her ring. I can just make out what it looks like, an eye of tiger stone, but intuitively, I know it's the tree, what's left of it. I shouldn't lean toward her, or allow her leg to glide against mine, recording the silky softness. I shouldn't encroach on her thoughts… but her mind is as open to me as she is bare.

"But more importantly, I refuse to admit my taxed imagination creates a phantom I'm more drawn to than I was ever drawn to Mike, or anyone else I dated. 'If you were real, I'd stay… Although you can't be, I wish you were.'"

We break away, and the spark I feel isn't in the air but my trousers. When I gas, she grabs for me, and I steady her for a long minute, understanding her life and her world, her fears and desires, her loneliness that has undoubtedly matched mine. I feel the need to apologize, but I want to know more about her, so I cinch her to me. "I didn't mean to intrude. You okay?"

"I'm glad you're here, and I'm better than okay. I feel like all my life, something has led me here. I think that something is actually…you. I feel a catharsis I didn't know I needed."

"Glad I could be of service."

"You're more than a servant. You're special, James. And I haven't had this much fun in a while. You make me feel *alive*. And you're a good teacher." She holds her head up high.

"You're everything to me. Beautiful."

"With you, I feel beautiful." She pauses for a beat. "But, I'm not quite Agnes without my locket, so I think we should head to the faux jewelers. I don't need the real thing to dress up."

A pain shoots through my chest, right where the locket lies in my breast pocket when she clutches her bare neck. I don't deserve this woman. Not after what I did—am doing—by continuing to keep from her information that will drive her away from me, which is the truth: she's dead. "S-sure," I sputter. "Let's check out one of the trinket stores."

CHAPTER 5

Emily

"I haven't been in this store since before I was pregnant, but sexy cowgirl never goes out of style, right?" I almost smack myself in the head. Downer much? But my attempt to switch up my reveal must work because James pauses halfway to the Pink Door Boutique.

"I never wanted children, and then when I did, it was too late."

His somber tone rips my heartstrings, and I lift

my hand, placing it against his stubbled cheek that feels warmer than it did earlier. Do I dare prod into his personal life?

Rolling my palm against his mouth, he kisses me. "If I could do it all over again, perhaps I'd get a chance to do things differently."

With a flick of my gaze, I regard this regret-filled man. By the fine lines near his eyes, he appears to be mid-thirties, but not more than a decade older than me. "James, if you want children, there's still time to find someone, fall in love, settle down, and make babies."

James doesn't add to the subject, and I'm not one to push. Still, when it comes to having another child, I'm still in my twenties and healthy. I still have a chance to start again, to feel the flutter of life inside of me, the excitement of mothering a newborn. And, in the back of my mind, though I shouldn't stoke the vision, I picture what James' and my child would look like. Definitely blue eyes, skin that easily sunburns, and dark hair with auburn threads twined within the strands.

"You want to share what's making you grin?" James holds the door open.

Do I? "I'm just happy you're here with me, and I hope you are, too."

"Very."

As I pass the threshold, I take note of the door. I always loved old doors, and I supposed the store gained its name due to the entry's double doors. Multiple layers of peony-pink chipped paint hang off the old wood so thick, I'm surprised the rusty hinges hold the panels upright. I find the outside has a whimsical and inviting feel, but I also wonder about the building's history. If the door could talk…

James adjusts his cravat necktie, seeming to enter the shop with caution, even going so far as to check behind us.

"Is everything okay?"

I follow James' gaze to a woman leaning against a building across the street. Dressed in a long-sleeve shirt and a floor-length skirt, she's curvy and pretty. Her hair lies tight to her scalp, accentuating her oval face and deep-set eyes. "Do you need to talk to her?"

"No. I'll meet up with Jane later."

Jane. Yes, Calamity Jane, I recall from history books. "She's pretty."

"I'm struck blind by *your* beauty."

I giggle as we head inside. "You make me feel, well, noticed, when Mike never did."

"He was a fool. After you..."

Inside has a more modern feel. Contemporary outfits hang on the walls. Several customers wander the space, while I head to the jewelry wall, James in tow. I make a mental note to return after the festival and try on some of the cute outfits.

One thing is true, if you're running your own store, in my case the antique shop, it's hard to check out others. I spot a sexy lace dress with see-through arms and legs. It's out of the ordinary for me to be drawn to this type of clothing, but what if I took a chance? "This place has a timeless feel. I mean, when isn't black fabric and lace desirable?"

"I prefer what you're wearing, and not Madam DuFran. Unless we're alone."

A flash of heat floods through me, and I shake my head, believing James is very serious in his opinions. He doesn't seem to hold back, whereas Mike never really let me in. "I'll remember that."

James keeps close but doesn't crowd me. I suppose it's the gown I'm wearing, lots of fabric billowing about the floor. Or the fact that every time we touch, a weird flashback overtakes my body. At least my head doesn't hurt, like the first time, as if I'm giving in to the vision, chasing after a memory I believe I lost.

Holding up a miniskirt made of fur, James closes one eye. "I prefer your style of clothing. These reveal too much skin and invite wandering eyes."

"Wandering eyes? What are you, from the turn of the century?"

"Depends on which one."

"Agnes' time. You really do play the part well."

James kisses me, taking another chance that I may experience one of my episodes. But the only thing that sways is my growing feelings for him. His touch lights up my body like fireworks, not the roadside Fourth of July stand tempered kind, but the big fireworks, the kind that will bombard the skies over Deadwood tonight at the peak of the Wild Bill Days' festival.

"Necklaces. Pick one, so we can make our way to the concert outside." He presses his hand against the small of my back.

I shudder as I feel warmth seep into me. Does he realize his closeness pleasantly sidetracks me? I slide around one rack, lifting my dress so the frilly edge doesn't catch. "If you stop distracting me, I can find a necklace sooner."

"Fine. No touching."

He holds up his hands as if I'm off-limits, when

my body actually craves his touch. It's the strangest sensation but reminds me of stories passed down through our family. "Did you know that the first time Agnes spotted Bill Hickok, she fell madly in love with him? Supposedly, he was a bit hesitant. She wasn't sure why, because he sent her love letters and respected her, even told her he was in awe of her business capabilities, running the circus. Then he gave her the locket. It has an inscription, but it's too worn to read. I do wish I knew what he wrote to her."

James scrubs his face and then meets my gaze. "I never knew that. I hope she understood how holding back could leave a guy confused. I didn't know whether she'd head overseas, so how could I commit. Although, she did appreciate jewelry now and then."

His first-person narrative throws me a bit, but then I am speaking candidly in public, and we're supposed to stay true to our parts. James, I fear, has committed to the role longer than he should. "You mean the real Wild Bill."

"Yes, of course. Wild Bill, the outlaw she tamed with her allure. I understand he also fell deeply in love with her."

I wish I could tell my ancestor that James loved

her at first sight. I'm not sure I believe, but something about James has me wishing instalove is true. However, I wonder if Agnes held back because she doubted the sincerity of his feelings, since he bebopped back and forth between states, as well as headed west to find gold so soon after they married.

"I, James Hickok, never doubted his intentions regarding Agnes. He loved her, wholeheartedly."

I run my finger through a string of necklaces, coming up with a bullet with an inscription. "Wild Bill Hickok 8-2-1876. Everyone knows Jack McCall shot Wild Bill with a single-action Colt .45 and not a .38. I can't believe they sell lies and get away with it. Right?"

James' face flushes. "You'd be surprised what people get away with."

Get away with, as in a white lie? As in a plotted affair? As if a light knock at the door of my mind, I let the vision of Mike with Noel inside. I wonder how long they went behind my back, spending time after hours to linger. Or had they coupled after I ended our engagement? "Let's move on. I need a necklace. Without one, I feel as if I let my ancestor down in the fashion department, not to mention losing her locket."

"It was an accident. I'm sure she'd forgive you."

Would she? Does an accident make the loss any less forgivable? I lost something precious—my daughter and my mother, generations wiped from this world. If Mike embraced our future in Deadwood, embraced me and our love, would he have listened to me when I raised my voice in warning a second before the collision? I'll never know, I guess. "James?"

"Yes?"

"Do you have anyone special in your life? Have you ever been in love? And if so, how did you know?"

He grumbles and raises his hand, stroking his mustache. "A long time ago. It's just a feeling that I can't explain, other than it is one of mutual compassion, forgiveness, and admiration in every moment. I'm hopeful to find that again."

When he glances my way, his gaze is liquid blue, the color of deep oceans. I float my head against his hand that he places flush across my cheek. I want a deep relationship, but I'm not ready for one yet. I don't want to jump into something I'll regret. I wouldn't want to be someone's temporary rebound. But I am having fun with James and, every time he touches me, warm tingles ripple through me, encouraging me to consider if he *could* be more. Not a rebound, but a forever. "Me, too."

James motions to a jewelry stand on top of the counter. "How about those?"

We weave our way through the clothing displays toward the counter. There are silver and gold chains, stone pendants, feathers, and flowers trapped in resin. I spot a gold chain with a dangling nugget pendant, which I hold up to my neck. "What do you think?"

"Is that the one you want?"

His frown doesn't surprise me, as if I know how he's going to react before he actually does. "You don't like it?"

He lifts the nugget to his mouth and attempts to sink his teeth into the replica. "This isn't real."

I'm laughing before I can stop myself, a big, opened-mouth laugh, like Julia Roberts. "Oh my God, James, how are you not taken?"

"Who'd take me? I haven't done anything wrong. This gold nugget isn't real and shouldn't be displayed as so."

He pulls back and folds his brows over those beautiful eyes. Now I'm laughing harder. Sometimes he says things that don't put him in this time, but I remind myself that the store crowds by the minute. Several other customers seem to be amused, giggling under their hands.

I rise up on tiptoes, because he's just that tall. "Why are you single?"

"I'm looking for someone special. Someone like Agnes. Agnes."

Knots form in my throat because I fantasized about my family history and the relationship between the two for years, wondering, yearning for a love like theirs. What if I could be Agnes to James? "She waited for him for five years, never knowing if he was living or dead, except for occasional correspondence. She loved him and him only until the day he died. I think wanting what they had is okay. Why settle and never get what you really want, what you deserve? So, as much as I hate being alone, I understand, James. I really do. I'll never settle again."

"I believe you. I loved my wife very much. She'd never settle just to fill a hole."

His admission stings, but I scold myself. He's opening up, and I'm grateful he feels comfortable enough to share his loss. Whether they divorced or she died, his sorrow is palpable. "Thank you for sharing. It's not easy moving on…"

His thumb across my cheek has an endearing feel as I smile up at him.

"Thank you for this…"

I'm assuming he's talking about the realness we're sharing, and with that, I finger other pendants, deciding on a brooch, a simple gold half-circle with sapphire gems and pearls, which I hold up to my lapel. "I like it with this dress, and it's affordable, since the gems and pearls are synthetic."

With a somewhat approving look, James nods. "You deserve the real thing."

"I'm not so sure. The locket wasn't meant for me. It's irreplaceable, which is why I want to find it as its meaning represents something permanent and true."

"Did it, now?"

"That's what I'm told…"

James pays as I affix the brooch to my dress, the sapphires more or less blending with the gown. But, the more I think about the locket, the more I'm pulled to find it. "I'd like to check out the pawn shops around town. Maybe someone found the locket at the accident—"

"Accident?" The cashier rings up the purchase. "You mean to tell me some lowlife stole your jewelry at the scene?"

"I can't be sure and don't want to jump to conclusions, but Mt. Moriah was the last time I saw it."

Her eyes widen as she leans across the counter. "Where the woman died? Oh, my God, what a piece of shit. If I hear anything, I'll let you know if you give me your name."

"Em—" I stop myself. I don't need anyone involved in my personal business or getting riled up over misinformation. "Agnes. Agnes Hickok."

"Of course. I recognize you now. In the meantime, my aunt owns a pawn shop on Deadwood Street. You might want to check there, or accept that it's lost forever."

My heart falls at the thought while James is retrospective, and for good reason. He turned beat red, balling his fists. I wasn't the only one who noticed his rage. "I can take care of myself, James, but I do appreciate you wanting to fight the person who stole from our family. Your response is chivalrous, and, frankly, a turn on."

My words fall out before I cover my mouth, flushing.

"A turn on, hey?"

Too embarrassed to speak, I nod. I need to remind myself I'm not Agnes, even though I'm pretending. I'm not living a fantasy. I'm not married, dating, or sleeping with James. Yet.

Together we stroll back out into Main Street,

the flow of people whipping around us as if they're running from a horned bull. I take a glance behind me to make sure I'm safe, but James pulls me against him just as a cowboy, pistols raised, tucks into the alley. "Is that guy part of the production cast?"

"Don't give him or anyone else another thought. The only place that man's rushing to is a dead end. Better to pick our way carefully, enjoy these precious moments, don't you think?"

Hand in hand, I can't argue. The sun radiates warmth on my face, the music's beat keeps a slow tempo with each step I'm taking, and calmness rolls over me that wasn't there before. The relaxing stroll gives me time to smile and nod, to meet the friendly gazes of passersby. When I spot the woman who looks like Giana—one of my sorority sisters from UCLA—I raise my hand. "Giana! Giana! Giana?"

I drop my hand, feeling embarrassed.

James squeezes my shoulder. "The music is loud. Probably still deaf from the booming sound system."

I watch as Giana trots to the opposite side of the street, meeting up with a friend. "Yeah, sure. Maybe she didn't recognize me in the dress. I just wanted to introduce you to her. We were best friends in college before she had to drop out and I lost contact. I haven't seen her in years."

"Another time, perhaps."

My gaze lingers on Giana, but a wave of dizziness overcomes me. I think to ask James about the spell, but then I stop myself. It's as if I'm invisible.

James tightens his grip. Is he holding me against him because he senses my lopsided connection to Deadwood and the people, to this moment in time? Or is something else seriously wrong, a result of the accident?

The episode seems to pass as quickly as it came, but then another curve ball swerves in my direction. Giana jogs toward me, staring right past me, right through me and James.

CHAPTER 6

James

Before Giana can breeze straight through us, I roll Emily in the opposite direction, closer to the storefronts, kicking my ass all the way to the curb. What the hell is wrong with me? This was my chance to console Emily when she comes to terms that she's not of this world. Instead, I'm playing along like everything about this veil is hunky-dory.

"Well, that was embarrassing. I guess I should dress up more often, so people recognize me instead of avoiding the crazy lady."

Only she's not crazy. There's nothing wrong with her memory. She's dead, and with that, some memories are stuck in a freeze frame. "Happens to me all the time," I lie, and, for the first time, I consider telling her the truth.

Of course, I don't. I don't want her to leave me when I'm enjoying reacquainting myself with my wife. Don't I deserve to spend a day with her? A solid day, where nothing goes wrong, and we are free to love and laugh and live?

I regain our leisurely stroll as the tension drifts, and Emily pauses at each storefront window, peering at the displays, tooled leather belts and shoes, coffee cups with my name emblazoned on the sides, key chains and finger towels, shirts with hoods built right into the collars…

"Of course, people know you. You perform as Wild Bill. Naturally, the friends you made all recognize you."

As if on cue, Charlie Utter beelines toward us. He's a plainsman, scout, merchant, and one of my good friends. Seeing him formally dressed, my heart clenches, his ritualistic tidiness apparent even in death. How long has it been since my friend buried me, though he tried to save my life a million times over from my excessive drinking and gambling?

I'm a damn fool, breaking my own rule and turning my back to the open door the day I was shot dead, as if I encouraged Jack McCall's vengeance. But I ask myself, why is my comrade here? Will Charlie chastise me again? Is he here to warn me that keeping Emily here will gravely cost me my soul? Hers?

No. I'm here to guide her. To show her true love exists.

"My pard, J.B., you didn't tell me Agnes arrived. When? How is it possible I was so busy to miss such grace and beauty, just as you described her?" Charlie lifts Emily's hand and plants a gentle kiss on top.

"Oh, my." Emily bats her lashes against pinking cheeks.

"I'm Charlie Utter, a bit of a sidekick to J.B., here. It's a pleasure to meet you, Mrs. Hickok."

Emily blushes even more as she dangles her hand until Charlie releases her. "Oh, I'm not really his wife—"

"As Deadwood doesn't yet have the means to recognize legal decisions," I interject.

Charlie spies me derisively. "Bill, you must teach her the rules, if you plan on keeping her here. Otherwise, your time here together will be short-lived."

Emily must catch on or consider Charlie's

threat because she takes up my hand, giving me a squeeze. But again, I order myself not to interfere as it's imperative for Emily to piece together the rules of this veil, as well as the lawlessness of the old Deadwood, where loose rules were rarely followed, I remind myself. Even my killer hunts me as we speak. "How long are you here?"

"Not long. May we talk privately? Briefly?" Charlie motions to an alcove in the building.

Emily steps aside, and wouldn't you know it, she's checking the storefront window of Deadwood Alive, the reflection revealing not her, but the strip of green grass and trees from the opposing elementary school.

"Why don't you check out the shop? I'll only be a minute," I encourage, but she declines with the shake of her head.

"I'll only be a moment." As I excuse myself, Charlie takes my elbow in urgency. "What's going on that can't wait until tomorrow?"

"McCall's gunning for you. You don't have much time."

"He's always threatening. Let him come."

"I don't know. Something feels different. I'm heading out of town—have letters to deliver—but I'll be back to check on you..."

I shake Charlie's hand, pressing my palm against his and holding on longer than I should, believing this is the last time I'll see him. I can't help but miss our adventures, even though my friend tried to keep me straight. "Then it's a bitter good-bye, my friend. I wish you well."

"Enjoy your time together." Charlie tips his hat to Emily as he ambles past.

But this moment repeats itself as I watch him stroll away. Pain twists deep in my gut that this day is the final time my good friend will stand in my presence.

Damn strong is the urge to truck after him, to catch a glimpse of my pard fading into the light, or straight out disappear that I stagger and catch myself. He's not real. Nothing is, though everything about this moment feels permanent.

Emily takes up my hand, watching as Charlie disappears into the crowd. "I'm sorry you can't spend more time with Charlie. I can tell by the way he regarded you that he cares for you very much. And I understand loss. I miss my mom. She died recently. I'd give anything to converse with her again." She holds her belly down low.

And I know what she's thinking as she stares blindly into the throng of families. I miss my unborn child. I pull her against me, her contact soothing me instantly when she leans into me, but how screwed up is that? "Let's spin this sullen mood."

"I agree. We were having fun today no matter what. Have you ever seen Reba in concert? She's an amazing singer. I saw her in..."

Emily's reciting facts about the star vocalist who's led her followers to Deadwood, while I'm figuring out my next move. Sure, I've heard of the singer, but I'm focused on Emily. How long do I have left here before she realizes the participants grooving to the music are not mortal? How long before self-preservation and duty requires me to defend myself from an apparition that's sure to both shock and spook the crap out of Emily when Jack kills me again? Again and again.

"Stop right there or you're a dead man."

Well fuck.

Emily grips my arm, but I shove her behind me, putting her between my back and the storefront as I whirl around. Is this fun outing with Emily actually a dangerous display? 'Cause shit's about to go down. "Son of a rat's ass. Davis Tutt, you better stand down if you know what's good for you."

"We don't want any trouble." Emily holds out

her hands, checking me out of the corner of her eyes.

Play it down. Don't overreact. Lull Emily into believing this all for show. I wink in her direction, hoping she catches my hint.

"Tutt, I don't want any trouble. So, whatever is bothering you, I'm sure we can talk it out."

Murmurs from the bystanders gather, locking me and Davis in a circle of spectators.

"I'm done talking. It's time for killing. You won the last round, but I'll be damned if you'll win this one." Tutt waves Emily to the side. "Pretty lady, you better make your way over to me, if you want to live."

She jams her hands on her hips, giving me a sassy smile. "I most certainly won't. Now this has gone too far." She yanks my arm. "James, I don't want any part of this."

I shake her off, damn pleased she's playing along, but this isn't time for pretending. Plus, I don't need her breaking into hysterics while Tutt, the bastard, has been haunting me for what feels like a millennium. I warned him the first time, and all the quick-draw duels in between. "Unless you want to die all over again, I suggest you go about your business."

Davis rocks, lifting one foot off the ground and then the other as he hovers his hands over his guns. "Not until I get my gold watch back. I won it fair and square."

As if muscle memory overtakes my palms, I shadow my weapons. "Maybe, maybe not. If I recall, I warned you not to go flashing the timepiece around. Instead, you bragged about winning and devalued what I held dear. I won't stand for no braggart."

Tutt flicks his wrist, and, in a blur, he fires, the discharge resounding between the buildings that flank Main Street, and onlookers scatter like chickens in a henhouse that's infested by coyotes.

I'm knocked back several inches, both my pistols hot and smoking from my quick action, while I wrestle to conceal the hole punched through and through, right over my ethereal heart.

Emily screams and grabs me by the arms, as my pants seem to be missing my legs. I never lose focus as my vision blurs and then blackness teases my peripheral. Son of a bitch, Tutt shot me. While I struggle to regain my faculties, the scattered onlookers waddle back, again gawking.

"Oh my God. James, are you hit? Hurt?"

With fervor, she's digging through my clothing,

running her fingers through my long hair and searching for a flesh wound, when that fucker shot me through the heart.

Of course, Emily won't come up with a dash of crimson because I don't bleed. She doesn't bleed. Still, I feel a pain and tightness in my chest just as I spot Tutt, head bowed and weaving. Fuck, that could have been me.

Pull it together. Straighten up. If I can't get Emily to believe this is truly a ruse, she'll know I'm not real, and I'm not ready to let her go just yet. "Just a show, Pet. Nothing but smoke and mirrors."

"Boys, I'm killed..." Tutt drops and several hustlers rush to his aide, carting the sorry bastard away.

I'm not focused on Davis any longer, though. Finding sturdy ground, I force myself to look away from the hole in my shirt, which I roughly cover. How the hell has his bullet pierced the spot right where my heart used to lie, as if Tutt and I have suddenly changed places? "Well I'll be damned, Davis got off a bullseye this time."

Wild eyed, I can see Emily's trying to make sense out of the fact I'm still standing.

"This time? You mean he actually shot you."

Think of something quick. "Just a play, darlin'. Nothing to worry about."

She smacks me in the arm, and her blue gaze narrows to pins. "I thought you were actually shot. I thought… You could have been killed."

"This is the Wild West, but it's nothing but a stunt Tutt and I rehearsed a million times."

She bats me away, brooding, and she has every right. Tutt came out of thin air, and I ask myself why here, why now? Clearly, if I were alive, I'd be as dead as a fish in the desert, drying out to nothing but bones. "Emily."

"Don't speak to me. I'm mad at you." She huffs, folding her arms as we continue making our way up town. "That was too real for my tastes."

Yeah, she's pissed, as pissed as Agnes was the day I decided to leave her and return west, even though we knew the outcome of striking it rich would embellish our future. Neither of us was ready to part ways, exactly, but I was a near vagrant for half the previous year, and, if I wanted to give Agnes the life she deserved, I needed to find a lucrative way to ensure our future.

Emily wrestles from my grasp as I attempt to pull her against me, landing stiff against my side. "I'm sorry. I was a fool. I should have waved Davis off more forcefully."

"Promise me you'll never do that again."

"Are you worried about me?"

"No. You're a grown man I only just met. If you want to play the fool, that's on you." She roughly wriggles free.

"You *are* worried about me..." I roll her into me the moment I see her grin, and I press my lips to hers, igniting the buzz of magic we possess when we touch.

She breaks contact, breathless. "Does your seductive charm work on all the ladies?" she chides.

"I'm not interested in anyone but you."

"James, I know we just met, but I don't want to lose you."

She kisses my cheeks, my lips, not like a woman I only encountered, but like my wife. And I fall hard. Although I shouldn't make promises, I stare into her eyes and promise her the world. "It's okay. I'm here. I'm not going anywhere. Promise."

She slips her hand into mine, and we dive into the sea of listeners.

Up ahead, the stage comes into view. Hands raised and boots stomping, the crowd roils.

We flow around one body after another, and not all of the bodies are ghosts. Making sense out of the humans I can see escapes me. I have no tie to them that I know of. Yet, there must be a reason, some way I will affect them in the future, just as Emily has a connection to Giana.

"I'm worried I'll get lost, so hold me tight," Emily shouts over the rumble of drums, guitars, and lyrics.

"I have you." And I do. I carry her very soul in my hands. I don't want to let her go, especially now that I sense she cares about me. Worries about me.

I lead her toward a narrow railing that borders the temporary stage. The country singer is petite, middle-aged, with short fiery-red hair, singing about life beyond here. I realize the verses of "Is There Life Out There" seem more applicable now than ever before. To live for today, you gotta do something foolish and crazy, maybe similar to the stunt pulled by Davis Tutt just a few moments ago. So, I take a reckless chance. "Do you trust me?"

"Yes. Of course."

I leap onto the railing, using my free arm as a balance, while I offer to take her hand. "Join me."

"I can't. Not in this dress. I'm not a tightrope walker. I'm not really Agnes."

I hesitate for a beat. She's my wife, the woman I believe in. "Oh, but you are if you believe."

A high-pitched whistle captures my attention, and the man who waves us forward isn't mortal at all. "Here's her chance to learn the truth," I mutter, just as she slides her palm into mine, and I quickly discover I own two left feet.

As I teeter, maneuvering myself along the bar, she masters it like it's second nature. "You're good at this. Always held natural abilities since the first time I—"

What? Spotted her performing in the circus tent? "You're a natural, Emily."

Emily trots on the beam, teasingly. "The trick is not to stay in one moment too long. Don't think. Just let your feet take flight."

While I wrestle with my boots on the four-inch bar, I find it's my heart that has wings. And I'm soaring as I pull her onto the stage. Her words are exactly what I longed to hear—don't think, just do. I need to get out of my head as much as anyone whose past haunts them. I need to live.

I grip her hand, keeping focus on those beautiful blue eyes staring up at me. I'm sure as shit not going to screw up my time with her, however short. I slide my hand to the small of her back, cinching her to me. Maybe this is my chance to right my wrongs. Save her soul. At least one of us is savable. "Will you dance with me?"

"For the rest of my life, making new memories.

Now, kiss me like you'll never leave me. Dance with me until we're the only ones still dancing and the moon is high in the sky."

I can't believe what I'm hearing. Before I overthink what I'm about to do, I'm leaning forward, making contact with her lips, tangling up in her embrace as she draws me down even more.

Feet pounding to the beat, that gown of hers swishing on the temporary stage, I swing her around until the muscles in my legs burn, until I'm wringing with sweat as the music reaches the crescendo of the encore performance. And all I can think about is stripping Emily free of the dress and making love to her until the rooster crows. "God, I want you."

She laughs, tipping her head back to reveal her lean, kissable neck.

"And I want you. In fact, I'm done with your seductive teasing tonight." She rises on tiptoes, grazing her lips against my ear. "I can feel you want me, while I might just come undone right here on stage, and Madam DuFran would be proud."

I wiggle my brows and bust out laughing. "She would for sure, and I'm not one to disappoint."

Without another word, Emily leads me off the stage as we take in the moonlit walk, so enamored with each other on our way toward the hotel, our measured steps become urgent. I don't pay attention to the shadows, though I should. I don't hear the murmurs of vengeful outlaws. Emily, if she spots Mike and Noel scurrying from the car into the Celebrity Hotel, keeps her mouth, hands and gaze on me.

By the time we reach the elevator, I'm well on my way to setting her corset bindings free, and she's removed my cravat and unbuttoned my sack coat and shirt. The door to the room is a weak barrier as she throws a dangerously seductive look over her shoulder.

"Are you ready for me, James? Because I'm ready to be claimed. Claimed by the outlaw."

CHAPTER 7

Emily

James kicks open the suite's door, lifts me, and I squeal. Never have I found so much flirty fun as with this man. Every single person he introduced greeted me with love and warmth, reminding me I belong here. Deadwood is my home. But James makes me feel wanted in a way I never imagined. I can't believe I'm falling for him, or that I'm about to have sex with him on the first date. "Thank you for tonight. It was magical."

"The night's just getting started, and I plan on making it *very* memorable." Once through the door, he closes it with his shoulder, pausing briefly to lock it.

He owns my lips, taking the lower between his teeth, drawing a giggle from me as he sucks. "James, you make me feel like I belong with you. I can't explain it, but you make me feel so good."

With a bounce, he flings me onto the downy comforter, but he doesn't climb over me as I expect. Flecks of steel gray catch the light in his dark-blue eyes. He's gorgeous, and his wicked, possessive grin brims with power I desperately crave. I pat the comforter, encouraging him with a seductive smile to join me. "I won't bite."

"I will." The bed shakes when he kneels beside me. "I'm gonna make you feel so good, darlin,' you'll never leave me again."

Again… Have we been here before? Made love? Is my accident causing me to forget sections of my life? Either way, in the back of my mind, I hope he's right. James watches over me, but is his scrutiny one of desire? Suspicion? Distrust? Or is he as afraid of me leaving him as I am of him abandoning me? Is that why we've been inseparable since we met? Maybe I don't care. "I'm not going anywhere without you. I promise, James."

He lands his mouth on mine, and his savage kiss is as desperate as it is filled with a passion I'm hungry for. He cups my head and rolls on top of me. The weight of him is bliss, locking me under him. As if muscle memory, I encircle his taut hips, cinching my ankles around them. I want him too, the feel of his skin sliding against mine until we're both sweaty and panting, until we're both completely sated.

When he breaks away, he flanks my head with his arms. "You're perfect. Beautiful. I could kiss you forever."

I nod in agreement, but we both know the truth. Nothing is permanent. No one is perfect. This night has a time limit, and, in the back of my mind, I'm not sure if James is real. I don't care. "Promise me you'll make tonight last. I want to show you how much you mean to me, because I'm falling for you, James. I'm head over heels in love with the sheriff, the gunslinger, the gambler, the outlaw. I never believed I could feel this way about anyone. But it's you. I think it's always been you my heart's searched for. Now that I found you, I'm never leaving Deadwood."

He leans in, briefly, placing his forehead against mine. "I needed to hear that. I don't want this night to end, either. So let's stretch out our time together. Let's slow things down."

His fingers are long and thick, but he works magic with my dress' buttons, sliding each free of their bindings in slow, pleasurable seconds. He glides the straps off my shoulders, lowers his head as he plants kisses on my collarbone, drawing out a shudder.

I'm sure I moan, but I'm too lost in sensation to know if the one groaning is me or him. "You did this before."

Moving behind me, he unlaces the corset, which gives him a challenge. "Just like you to make me wait for what I'm wanting: you naked, squirming under me, submitting, and the two of us coupled as husband and wife."

I'm not his wife, but I roll with it. It's the first time I admit to myself that I feel Agnes with me. Not only that, but I believe she's always been part of me, searching for someone. There is calmness inside of me but also joyful anticipation. She's wanted James as much as he's wanted her. But I'm her and she is me, as if our souls are eternally entwined. Admitting the knowledge definitely throws a twist. I release the tension in my body, settling into the feather-topped bed as I welcome her into my very soul. "I want to feel everything with you, and I don't want to make either of us wait a second longer. I want to be James' Agnes."

"Emily…"

"She wants him too. So very badly."

He trails his hands across my silk bra, the fibers snagging on his callouses and turning me on. Everything about his ruggedness calls to my soul, his scruff that bites at my neck, his mustache that brushes my nipples. Nipples that he devotes his time to, pinching and rolling the sensitive pebbles through the cloth until I'm soaked and he is so very hard against my thigh.

"I didn't expect black." He lifts a brow.

"It matches my panties and, now that I'm closer, the flecks in your eyes."

I slide my hands over his shoulders, recording their symmetry, their strength, as I work my way down to his taught waist. He's mature, solid, and the extra bulk sends spasms through my core. Before I can think if I *should* take control, I'm removing his trousers, exposing the mast that's hard and waiting to sail.

"Don't ask me to stop," he rasps.

I shake my head, as I wrap my hand around his girth, stroking the sleeve of skin over his firm length. I roll my thumb over the tip and find a droplet of dew waiting. "Never."

He can't know how much I want to be loved, staked, and claimed. He can't know that he's the type of man I waited for and wanted since that first time I saw him pull Mike from the flames. James is a hero in my eyes. "Will you be a gentleman when you make love to me?"

He barely raises his head from trailing kisses down my belly. "You own the show tonight, darlin.' I can be as good or as bad as you want. Tell me what you want."

I thread my fingers through his hair, tugging where the strands are long, watching as they dangle through my fingers. "I want the outlaw."

Lowering his head, he groans as he crawls up my torso, kissing me long and slow, until my head spins and I writhe beneath him. He slips off my dress and panties, staring over my nakedness as if I'm a seven-course dinner and it's his last meal.

"You're beautiful, Emily. And I'm a very lucky man."

Lowering his head, he kisses my mouth, each cheek, my neck as he heads toward my breast. His magical tongue revs my desire, until I'm wet with an unrelenting need to take him into my body.

He switches from left to right, sucking, nuzzling his stubble against each breast until I'm panting, scissoring my legs against hips he rocks against my wedge. "I want you inside of me."

"Don't you know? I already am. And you're in me. Tonight is ours. Forever is our playground. And this devil is going to play hard."

I gasp, the sound full of want and need for this man. "James, I want you every way possible."

He reaches between our bodies, taking his length in his hand. He traces circles where I want him, and my core quickens.

"I'll tell you when to come," he orders

When he pushes his tip inside, I suck in a ragged breath.

He grits his teeth and his forehead dapples with perspiration. "You're made for me."

"And you for me."

Then James begins to move. His weight is heaven, his length delving deeper, touching places inside me that no man has reached. He's perfect, and he's mine. I can't let him go, believing we're made for each other, and he fills me to bursting, not only my body but my heart. "Harder, faster."

Between our bodies, he adds his hand, rolling his thumb over my most sensitive parts, circling, owning my body. He moves his hips, marching forward, retreating only to plunge deeper. "I don't want this to end. I want an eternity with you."

He moans. "Emily, I'd take you there if I could…"

The sound of my name validates his feelings for me. Not a memory of a wife long gone. Not of the spirit I'm sharing my body with, but me. I'm his, and he *is* mine.

Trailing that thought, my core flutters and then grips James, locking him inside me. Faster and faster he thrusts into me, but it's not pain I'm feeling as my body waits for his release; it's euphoria, it's bliss, it's heaven on earth.

"Come for me, Emily. Come."

He hurls me toward a blinding climax, sending me to the edge of ecstasy, and when I peer over the edge, he pushes both of us right over into a depthless gorge.

* * *

James

"James, you make me feel…"

I stroke Emily's face as her voice fades. I kiss her cheek, finally settling my lips against hers in a long, slow kiss as we both unwind. Our bodies grow heavy against the mattress. I admit that was the best orgasm I ever had, or maybe I forgot what being with a woman feels like after a hundred and fifty years. Either way, I'm floating, dozing, riding the buzz of ecstasy.

She nuzzles her head in the crook of my arm, her soft mews turning into softer sounds of dreamlike breathing.

I snug her against my bareness, knowing damn well what we share is shit, as long as I keep up the pretense of lying to her about who she really is, and that the bond we share is only as real as she's believing. Truthful words don't form on my lips, though.

I'm not real. She's not real. We are two souls living in the same veil, having found each other because the locket I gifted Agnes so very long ago binds us somehow. I can't reach in and pull Agnes out of Emily because the two are one, fused souls, one indistinguishable from the other. And I'm falling for Emily just as hard as I once loved Agnes.

"I want it to be you...forever."

I freeze against her, hearing her pledge and unsure if she's really asleep, if she's really talking about me. I have a decision to make, a choice I find more difficult than killing outlaws or fighting off a bear, harder than surviving the Civil War, worse than leaving Agnes when I headed to find our fortune, so we could live a happy life, a happy future. More painful than watching her waving and growing small as I rode off toward Deadwood.

With those challenges came hope, but telling Emily the truth—that I brought her here, that she's dead… How will we survive the lie? I want her as much as I believe she wants me. So, I rock her gently as I stare at the beauty in my arms. She's so perfect, so strong, so—

Trapped.

Locked to this plane.

A plane she wouldn't retain any knowledge of if I didn't let my selfish wiles interfere in her mortal world.

What are you going to do, James?

My shame gouges a groove inside my heart, kicking dirt and regret.

I don't want to let Emily leave here, leave me. I want her to love me—forever. But I must come to terms with right and wrong. Maybe the reason I'm here is to set her free. To set Jane free. To set everyone I ever wronged free.

I spot my shirt on the bureau, a hole blasted

through the material, no doubt straight through my vaporous chest.

And I make a decision as painful as any I ever made. It's the only choice where a chance for me survives, and I can hold onto some semblance of honor as a good man.

Not the selfish man, I confess, I am and who I shun.

Emily drags her leg up mine. "Make love to me again."

I want to deny the kisses she's stamping on my shoulder. I should twist away, so she can't take me in her hand. I should crawl from the bed and beg her forgiveness.

Instead, I roll toward her, slink my arm under her back, and draw her underneath me. In lieu of making excuses for why I shouldn't take her again, I plunge into her wet, pulsating core, owning her, possessing her, locking us together until she calls my name. Until I call hers. Until she reminds me why I'm here, waiting for her, risking souls just to hold her one more minute, just to feel her touch and smell her scent, just to hear her tell me she's mine and that I'm hers.

To love her one last time, I risk it all, amplifying the stakes. And when I pull the last quiver of pleasure from her and I'm spent, void of demands and wrongdoings, I hope in the night I don't fade to nothingness. I pray in the morning I'll discover the strength to let her go.

CHAPTER 8

Emily

My body tingles as if I'm riding white, puffy spring clouds under a brilliant sun. It's a corny analogy, but waking up to find James sleeping so soundly, twined within his embrace, I'm struck with a thought. I don't just want a romantic relationship with him. I want all of him. I want the ending where we stride off together, like the kind of relationship the real Agnes and her husband once had.

I wiggle free and make my way to the bathroom…and freeze.

The shirt James wore last night hangs loose

over the back of the chair, the morning light spearing right through a hole in the shirt's breast pocket.

My belly flips and I cover my gasp as I pick up the shirt with trembling hands. I hold up the square of fabric, letting the light accentuate the seared bullet hole, which has gone straight through the linen.

But then I pause, checking over my shoulder. James' chest rises and falls with each languid breath. He's not gasping. His complexion isn't pale and robbed of blood. If Davis Tutt actually fired his weapon, which clearly happened as I witnessed the event, that would mean James was shot in the heart.

No one can survive a bullet through a vital organ.

I removed James' clothes last night, finding no sign of a bulletproof vest or wound.

If he was mortally wounded, he definitely wouldn't be sleeping. He'd be dead.

Ghost.

No. He can't be, which leads me to consider if I've finally cracked, as in, I've lost my mind, due to my accident. Sure, I've considered the slim chance that he's impossibly perfect because he's an illusion, but, as I plunge my finger through the hole, it's as real as real can be.

I narrow my gaze, in case I've missed something. At a minimum, there should be physical signs—wheezing, a cracked rib, and bruising.

But then I run my fingers over something oval and hard inside his pocket that I didn't notice before. A metal object. Did it prevent the bullet from impaling James?

I breathe a sigh of relief, thinking how lucky he was to possess an object strong enough to stop a bullet inside his pocket.

I dip my fingers into the pouch, and what I draw out knocks me backward.

It's my locket.

For a full minute, I clutch it in my hand and hold it over my heart. It's not dented. It has no signs of damage, other than the wear that has faded the inscription. It still has that tiny photo of—

James.

Dead.

While my mind spins scenarios of why the photo's likeness is so acutely close to my James, another thought rushes to the surface, obliterating the former. Why does *he* have my necklace?

All along, he knew I was searching for my link to Agnes, my heritage. Knowing that information, why did he lie about the necklace's location when he's had it all along? What else is he lying about?

My head spins in the same way it did the first time I spotted Mike with Noel as a feeling of deep betrayal blasts through me. I cover my mouth and my throat constricts. Will anyone ever love me for the right reasons?

James is behind me, his presence a solid, stifling force. "I thought you were too good to be true, and I was right."

"If I'm not real, then what am I?"

He's baiting me, but I already see where I'm heading. "A figment of my imagination."

"Go deeper. Who am I?"

"James Hickok."

"What am I?"

Admitting James is dead is admitting I'm insane, but I'm already feeling washed-up and bloated. "Dead. A ghost."

"If I'm a ghost, then what are you?"

"Ruined. Mental. Sick. There's no other explanation."

"No? You summoned me the day of the accident, in the bathtub, in your shop, and every time since. We are linked, irrevocably, by that necklace—the one I gave my wife. The one I gave you so long ago."

I don't know if he's telling the truth, but I'm too

starved for information to let go of this twisted nightmare. "I'm your wife, reincarnated."

"Again and again. I don't know how it's possible, but the locket links us."

How can an object link souls? How can this be real? Or is all that mumbo jumbo about a spirit world not so farfetched? "That would make it magical."

"Or our bond is strong enough to link our souls. You only wanted true love, and I only wanted my wife back. But I see my fallacy now. In wanting her, I locked her to this plane as much as I sealed you here. I lied to you to keep you with me, and I regret doing that to you, when I should trust you with the truth."

But I didn't want the truth. I asked for the lie, and I played along, I admit to myself.

"I wanted to tell you why I kept the necklace the first time I saw you."

Frozen, I should twist and squirm, but I'm, once again, stiff and locked to the floor. Anger at myself builds, fuming and about to explode. "Then why didn't you?"

"Anything I revealed would have made you feel worse, sadder. I didn't want to be the cause of your pain."

I almost laugh out loud. I should be focused on the fact that I'm arguing with a ghost; instead I'm just as selfish, focused on material things instead of the fact I'm destroying him with *my* pain of betrayal. I realize my anger at Mike kept me brooding and restless. "You know nothing about how I suffered. You didn't want to make *yourself* feel bad. If you cared about me—truly cared—you'd have returned my property, which leads me to my next question: How could you steal it from a dead woman?"

He drops his arms, clearly shocked. I don't trust him to tell me the truth, but still I ask, "If you're a ghost, then what am I?"

I feel his hair dust my head.

"You won't believe me."

I pivot, facing him. "You're talking about regretting lying to me, and you're still hiding shit from me. Try me. What am I? Insane? Sick? Dreaming?"

"Emily, don't make me do this. Please…"

I feel the air around us snap with electricity, and I'm not oblivious that there is some major metaphysical shit happening. At least, I think there is. I figure maybe I'm here to help *him* move on. Maybe then I'll wake up. "Stop holding back. If you want to move on, you have to make peace with the past, and that includes owning up to the reason you stole and lied."

James sidesteps me and plops onto the bed, sinking into the mattress as he holds his head in his hands. He won't look at me, but that's fine. Right now, I feel played. Even my palms are sweating from my building rage.

"Agnes—"

"Stop already." I give him a full eye-roll. "Leave that poor woman alone. Agnes has been dead for almost two centuries. James, this isn't about Agnes anymore. This is about the life and death of *us*, if there even was an 'us' to begin with."

Struggling to remain calm, the urge to slap some sense into him almost wins, but I hold back, acting like the lady I am as I begin roughly folding my clothes.

He stands, reaches out as if I'm a fly who's suddenly caught in his spider web, forcing me to halt my trivialities.

"Emily, there are things you don't understand. I'm falling for you, head over heels, and the decision before me isn't one I can easily swallow."

I drop the corset, the ties forming a knotted nest at my feet and tripping me up. "If you ever want a second chance, third, whatever, you have to be vulnerable and risk telling the truth, no matter what the outcome. You have to be willing to risk losing. And most of all, you have to be willing to accept the consequences."

He stabs me with his reddened gaze. "Even if there's a chance you'll understand, the truth will destroy you."

Making busy work of my clothing, I kick what's piled on the floor into a stack. I have experience with a one-sided relationship. It sucks. "I'm already destroyed. Can't you see that? Without honesty and trust, our relationship is nothing but a void. As it stands, if you don't spill what's on your mind in the next thirty seconds, I'm walking out that door and we're finished."

He crowds me more than I wish, his big blue eyes filling with tears. Hell if I know if he's genuine, though. He's known for his acting skills, and I observed him in action. Maybe he's just telling me he's a ghost to get something out of me. He's just too damn talented for his own good. "Just tell me."

"I have to show you."

He peels my hand open to reveal the necklace, and when he clasps the locket portion between our palms, the room spins as if a vortex of memories circles around us, and there's nothing I can do to stop the onslaught of horror that preceded the deadly crash.

"There's the cemetery." I jab my hand in its direction as I'm tossed back into the day of the accident. Mt. Moriah's narrow road leads to the parking area.

"How long will we be here?" Mike shifts gears that grind as we ascend the slope.

He isn't thrilled with our family trip to pay homage to our ancestors. He'd rather stay in town, bar-hopping and dancing. I'm eight months pregnant, so neither of his choices are agreeable, but earlier I bartered. He's taking me and Mom to Mt. Moriah Cemetery, and then I'll accompany him to his favorite bar. On the way, I catch a glimpse of several groups I assume are tourists, choosing to hike up the steep hill. Mike is at the wheel, and I'm riding in the passenger side. Mom's in the back. She always grows nostalgic when we're here. "You're quiet, Mom. Are you okay?"

"I wanted to find the right time to pass on a family heirloom. Never thought we'd be near the cemetery where your ancestor is buried, but if James Hickok met you, I'm sure he'd be proud that his granddaughter turned out to be as much of a romantic as he was, according to his wife. Now that you're having a daughter, it's time to pass on the locket."

My mom's open hand appears, resting on the center console. The locket is oval and gold, with a photo of James showing through the glass front, and inside a photo of James and Agnes. I pick it up and it shocks me, but I brush off the buzz as an incoming storm charges the air. "Mom, are you sure? You had this forever."

"Absolutely. I hope it brings you much luck in love as it has me."

I clutch it in my palm and glance at Mike. I shouldn't doubt his love for me. I'm pregnant with his daughter. I'm sure he'll make a great father, when he's not overseas on business. But then I wonder… would Mike be with me if I hadn't gotten pregnant? Would he stay after our daughter is born, when he spends more time with his boss, Noel, than he does with me?

Suddenly, the locket seems to electrify, and I have a strong urge to bring it to my lips. I shouldn't kiss the image of James. I shouldn't desire a connection to a stranger, but a thought lingers: The truth will set you free…

Mike's truth? My truth? Where is my James?

A man appears, standing in the center of the lane as Mike swerves, but it's too late. The man's ethereal form slams into me with such force that I lose my breath.

Voices inside my head multiply, and I can't hear what the man is saying over the slush of others, but I feel a sense that he's warning me to stop the car.

"Mike. Stop. Stop!"

"Why? Parking is up ahead."

"Look out!"

Mom shouts behind me, but the impact jolts my head against the glass, which shatters. Blackness wraps me in its embrace. Seconds or hours may pass, but consciousness returns slowly and sirens wail in the distance.

People shout as chaos overtakes the scene, glass and the smell of smoke rise, ripe in the air.

I'm slumped forward, the seatbelt taught against my swollen belly. But out of the corner of my eye, I spot the man. No. James. He's tugging Mike from the driver's side.

"Mom?"

I'm met with a deafening silence.

"Mom?"

"Emily. I'm here. Please hold on… Please…"

Mike's at my door, his head bleeding a thick trail from his hairline, but then I'm free and in his arms. My hand rests limp across my belly. "The baby? Is our baby okay?"

My head throbs and I feel a cold chill infuse my veins and my teeth chatter, but I fight past the pain. "Where's Mom? Get her out."

Mike looks past me, but then Mom's beside me, tears pouring down her cheeks.

I must be bad off, because Mom forces a weak smile— a smile I noticed before, the one that always precedes bad news. And I just know. I'm not going to make it. So, I tell her the truth. I don't want her to worry about me. "Let go, Mom. I'll be okay. Let go…"

The last thing I see before I'm pulled into the darkness is the locket, held in the stranger's hand, arms he has outreached toward me as, strangely, I'm floating above the entire disastrous scene.

I shake the vision. The necklace is solid in my hand, as if breaching reality into my dreamland. What was that? How am I able to catch a bird's-eye view of the wreckage, of my mom on the gurney, of Mike near my body? Of James glaring up at me. But the memory can't be right. It can't. "I thought you were a Good Samaritan, but now I'm not so sure."

"If Agnes didn't reach out to me, everyone in that car would be dead."

A lightbulb goes off in my mind at my revelation that James' obsession with death is what keeps him here. But it's my fixation to avoiding the truth that keeps me restless, frustrated, and angry. "I don't know what role you played. But I do know your presence took everything away from me—my mom and my baby. It's your preoccupation with Agnes that bothers me the most. If you don't release her, everyone around you is doomed, I fear."

He balls his hands as his face flashes beet red.

Behind his dark gaze, I wait for him to explode, yell, or perhaps punch the wall as he watches me swinging the necklace around my finger.

Blowing out a long breath, he dips his shoulders. "Everyone who comes to Deadwood lives in the past or wants to, including you. But we can't go back in time. We can't follow clues that lead us home because they're gone and we're trapped in a forest of illusion. We're all stuck here until we *choose* to free ourselves, until we stop lying, stop reaching for the unattainable. Until we accept facts and open our eyes. But I know what I need to do, and now's my time to do it."

His low sullen tone drives pain through me. I hear what he's saying, but his vagueness rubs me the wrong way. As eccentric as he is, could it be possible that *he* has some type of mental illness, and not me? "Are you listening? I'm tired of following your bread trail. You lied to me multiple times, and I want you to leave so you can't hurt me again."

"And I will. But, Emily, look around you. Your disappointment and regret is holding *you* here. Not me."

"That's not true. You're the one to blame for me losing my baby. Of wrecking my life. On top of the lying, you thieved, defrauded, and posed as a damn catfish."

"A what?"

I jab my finger his way. "You're a rule breaker

who disregards everyone you come across. People want to kill you because you're an outlaw. You're the one who holds onto Agnes. She's dead. She's gone, and there's no one like her, and she's not coming back ever again. Stop holding onto the past, to your self-blame and self-loathing. Let go and move on. I'm planning on doing the same." *If I only knew how…*

James glances at the necklace dangling between my fingers.

"I can't move on while you hold onto material possessions that link us together. And after falling for you, I don't want to go, even though I know it's the right thing to do."

Rushing into a relationship is exactly what I wanted to avoid. I take responsibility for falling for James and leading him on. I'm stupid. He's fierce in the way he idolizes those he cares for, as well as self-loathing, I believe. But the lying...

I need space. Time to figure out what's happening. "Fine. If this necklace is the problem, it's yours. Destroy it, so we can all be free of its spell."

While I place the necklace on the dresser, James grabs his trousers from the chair and retrieves a cell phone from his pocket, smacking it onto the dresser. "It's Mike's."

I snap it up, staring at the screen and the last text. "Remember when…"

The screen blurs and rage heats me up inside. It wasn't Mike who called me, but James. When I look up, James has disappeared, leaving our resolution hanging, and the necklace is missing.

I'm so angry, I open my mouth to scream, but only a sob chokes out of me. I chuck the phone and it splits in two when it hits the wall. God, I wish I could talk to my mom. I decide to do the next best thing, which only makes the tears fall harder. I dress and head to the cemetery.

Even on the drive, I spot couples, happy tourists, and families. Several times, I think I see James and a woman hiking up the incline. But it's not him. It can't be. He never was and never will be. I'm on my own, just like when I was with Mike.

I'm losing my mind, talking to myself as I mull over the events from the past two days. How much worse can my head injury and my life get? Is it too much to ask for the truth when all I wanted was to settle down in Deadwood, fall in love, and have a family?

I park and make my way up the rocky terrain, heading toward the gravesite, when I spot Mike, crouched.

What's he doing here?

He hates cemeteries, but I deduce he must be visiting Mom and our little girl.

"Mike?" He doesn't acknowledge me in the slightest as I come to stand two feet behind him, but then, as I read the headstone, why would he?

Loving Daughter & Mother
Emily Agnes Lyffe
1995-2020

* * *

James

All that remains of me is shadows and mist. I don't know if Emily's and my time together is over as I slip the necklace into Mike's pocket. It belongs to Emily, and soon she will be gone. Our tie is broken, not because of some magical piece of jewelry, but because I lied to her—for good reason, at the time.

I may never get her back, and I have to live with that. Most of all, I regret lying to her and not trusting her with the truth because that implies she's weak, when she is anything but.

I don't deserve her or her love, even if I pledge

to bury the selfish man I embraced only moments ago. To prove my love for her has changed me, instead of forcing our relationship, I decide right now to set her free. She can decide for herself—even if her choice no longer includes being with me.

So, I brush my lips against hers ever so softly and breathe her in, and then I tip my head back and allow myself to fade...

CHAPTER 9

Emily

Hot tears rain down my cheeks as I feel the lingering dusting of James' lips against mine, and then he's gone, and this time I think for good. But I can no longer deny the truth. He was right. I'm crushed, but I recall the hints he so clearly showed to me…

"…as real as the tears you're crying…"

"You don't belong here…"

"You'll never have what you want if you don't let go."

"Nothing but smoke and mirrors."

My earlier blame can no longer be held on him, when he raised his arms to catch me when I fell that very first day of the accident. I believe he appeared to save me. Save me from myself, if that makes sense.

James provided examples as well, putting in front of me people and situations, which I failed to see. He revealed the truth via his actions. I'm the one who refused to accept the truth. I know what's real now.

Where I thought I wanted to settle in Deadwood, now I accept I'm gone. Dead. Gone. I don't belong here anymore. I don't belong on earth.

A light from above obliterates the skyline, tugging me toward its whiteness, but I feel split. Something is holding me to this realm.

I blamed my ex for dragging me through the brambles of emotions, but as I stand close to Mike, here he is, crying over my gravesite and clinging to a picture of me.

My heart plummets as I recall the scene in Bullock's. "All this time, I thought I was alive, strolling Deadwood, and talking to you as if there was still a chance—a slim chance—we could reconcile or at least work our way through the loss of our baby. I didn't know, even though you tried to tell me that I'm ethereal. I'm so sorry."

Mike doesn't look up as he balances the photo in his palm. "I'm the one who's sorry. Believe me, I loved you, but it wasn't until you died that I realized I needed to change. I was stupid, but I have a second chance with Noel. I hope you find your peace, Emily. I hope you know you were loved so very much."

The pain of betrayal doesn't fade as quickly as I'd hoped, but I force myself to see the truth. I'm as much to blame as Mike for not fully communicating my feelings. Instead, I held back. Instead, I pretended everything was okay with our relationship, when it paled my expectations.

Fear of losing him kept me silent. I am no better than James. "It's my fault you pulled away. How could you trust me when I never fully gave myself over to you?"

"Don't say that. It was me. I put up walls, and I know that now. You wanted to come home, but this place isn't home to me. At least, it wasn't. I'm sorry I resisted. I didn't take time to get to know the people. But you were right, Deadwood is family. I blame myself for the accident. My resistance to paying respects to your ancestors unfairly held my attention from the oncoming car—" He sucks in a choked-up breath. "I would have spotted the distracted driver who broadsided us, if I'd listened to you. Although the sheriff assured me I'm lucky, I can't find much peace knowing you died."

I place my hand over my heart and sink beside Mike. James didn't cause the accident. He warned us of the oncoming car. But it was too late.

Mike can see and hear me because we are connected, I assume, by the photo. He hit James who appeared when I called him, and then our spirits collided. James didn't see me and then center himself in the roadway. He was as unaware of me until the last moment. It was an accident. An accident. How could I know that summoning a spirit would bring him forth? "It wasn't your fault. It was just my time. Me, my daughter, and my mom's time."

He doesn't stand as he stiffens his spine, and something in his lap makes a squeaking sound. I try to peer around him, but he's too hunched over and protective as if he's wrestling with his emotions.

"Emily, I didn't understand why I could hear you, see you, but now I think I do." Standing, he swivels to face me, looking at me with his sad, sad eyes, before he waves toward a car parked at the edge of the cemetery.

Two women emerge, one helping the other. Noel and my mom.

My heart thuds to the dusty ground. I'm so shocked, I can barely stay standing. "Mom? Mom!"

With my next thought, I'm beside her, but as I reach out, my translucent arms sweep right through her. "No. Mom! Can you hear me? Mom, I'm okay. I'm so glad you're not hurt. Mom…"

She doesn't respond, but she allows Noel to help her around to the trunk of the car, where they retrieve a spray of flowers and a wicker bird.

Eternal life. As much as I try, I can't smell the sweet lavender and roses and honeysuckle. I can't touch the dewy petals and crinkly ferns. Because I'm not supposed to be *here.*

Mom stays behind while Noel meanders the path through the headstones.

I'm trying to comprehend how Mom's alive. "All this time, I thought Mom told me to let go…"

Mike shakes his head. "No. *You're* the one who told your mom to let go of you, to live. She's alive and well, but the accident was only three months ago, and she still wears a boot, since she broke her leg as you can see."

I split my gaze between Noel and Mom, who sinks back into the car. "Why didn't you tell me the other night?"

"I couldn't. I was too upset. But Noel recognized the signs of your ghostly arrival. She's the one who encouraged me to make peace, to open my eyes and accept you're here for a reason. So, I'm here, Emily. I know it must be hard for you to take this in when you're powerless to change the past. I'm so, so sorry I couldn't save you in the end. I tried. I prayed. I prayed so hard. But then you surprised us all."

Mike twists, revealing what he's holding.

My heart explodes and the light behind me casts its glow on the most beautiful baby girl. "She's alive."

"Meet your daughter, Emily Agnes Williams. We call her Emmie…"

Of course. I choke up, my throat sprouting an aching knot.

"She's healthy and happy. Perfect. You lived long enough to give birth and saved our baby girl."

I must space out as I'm taking in the bundle he's holding. Trying to wipe away tears of joy and surprise, while my heart's shattered into a million tiny pieces. But then I glance at Noel, standing beside Mike, wiping her eyes with one hand while clutching her crystal necklace in the other. …and now our baby *needs* a mom.

"Noel." I glance at her, sizing her up, so grateful for this blessing of a woman. I soon realize she has an angelic look about her I hadn't recognized before. I clasp my hands around Noel's, feeling the weakest static exchange between us.

Noel pops her head up. "I can't have children, but, if it's okay, I'd like to be Emmie's mom."

I don't know what to say...

"Emily, Noel has been here for Emmie. She loves her and stayed up through the night when she caught a little cold. Noel insists on accompanying me to the baby's doctor appointments and refuses to go back to work until Emmie goes to kindergarten."

Mike chuckles, and it's a beautiful sound. He shares with me about all the ways Noel has helped him, and when she sidles up beside him, she has so much love in her eyes for my baby, and for Mike, I can't help but smile, even though I ache from my loss. "I can see Noel loves her."

"It's true, Emily. She loves me and our daughter as if Emmie is her very own."

Noel adjusts Emmie's beanie, little wisps of auburn hair peeking out. "It's by your example that I came to understand the importance and sacrifice of family. I never thought I'd be a mom. And I promise I'll tell Emmie about her birth mom, so she'll never forget what a loving person you were."

Mike pulls down the blanket, letting me look at our baby's tiny fingers and toes, as she punches at the blanket as if she's showing me how strong she is, and happy. She has a tiny nose like mine and dark-blue eyes, but there is much that resembles Mike, like his curly hair.

I glance over at Noel standing so quietly, so patiently, listening and accepting. I realize she'll be this way with our daughter. "Mike, tell Noel thank you. Tell her I trust her and wish her to be the best mom ever. If she ever has any doubts, she can always go to Grandma."

I check Mom, who's seated and patting her eyes. "I miss you, Mom. Every day. But I'll be waiting for you, waiting for all of you."

Emmie makes another sound, grabbing my full attention.

Mike peels the beanie off, revealing her perfectly round face and tiny ears.

I cover my mouth, trying so hard to bite back my tears of loss, tears of love, tears of regret. But I realize, in life and love, loss is to be expected—it's a season.

Mike pushes the tiny, squirming bundle toward

me, holding her out for me to touch her, as caution wars in his expression. "Take her."

The moment is bittersweet. I finally have a baby, but I can't wrap her in my arms like a mortal. I can't clutch her to my breast, can't nurse my little girl, can't bury my nose into the crook of her shoulder or draw in her baby scent or flip pages of her favorite bedtime story again and again, and I'll never get the chance to etch her bedroom door as I watch her grow into a young woman....

Fabric encroaches, brushing against my arm as Mike pushes her forward.

"It's okay. I have her."

I know he won't let go. Some things it's okay to hang onto tightly, I tell myself.

As I'm filled to bursting with love, I understand James better, and why he clung to the woman he loved with his whole heart and soul.

I cuddle my face against my daughter's, the scent of baby shampoo filling my senses. I kiss her pudgy cheeks, and more tingles exchange between us. Even without the necklace, I can tell we are connected. I can feel it, and by her widened eyes, I sense she knows I'm here. "I love you, Emmie. Don't ever forget how much. You're beautiful and strong."

"Like her mom. You both are independent and fighters. Ahh, Emily, all I can do is promise you that I'll never forget you. I'll never let our baby forget her mom."

But here's the thing. As Mike swaddles Emmie in her blanket, I don't want to be enshrined. I see the fault in that as I glance at my mom, who poured her soul into the antique store, the dust and heirlooms and past lives of others, without going after more and creating something new. And James, in the way he worshipped his wife.

I don't want anyone else to fill their days with regrets and assume they're powerless to make changes. I don't want anyone to put their life on hold, mourning me, when life awaits, either in the mortal world or hereafter.

Life is a temporary gift, but love?

Love is timeless. I believe that now.

The tether to the light strengthens, tugging me, tugging my soul as the ghosts of Deadwood gather.

And suddenly, even though I don't spot James, I feel him all around me, his warmth, his touch, his scent, his tender kiss on my cheek. "I don't know whether reincarnation is real, but, James, if it exists, I hope you find who *you're* looking for. I hope you share a long, long mortal life with her, a second chance, and forever thereafter."

James materializes before me, but I'm the only one who sucks in a shaky breath. He's my love, my soulmate, and I know that for certain. "You came…"

"I'm forever, your forever. I love you. Always…"

Filled with choking emotion, James' declaration wrecks me, as I fight back tears of desperation to cling to him, to cross that mighty void together and take up his hand.

But I must accept fate. At the moment, I decide. For me? I have the opportunity to exist where love waits with my soulmate, and I'm jumping.

Headfirst.

Into the abyss.

Never looking back.

For the last time, I twist, facing my daughter where I plant a kiss on my Emmie's cheek, exchanging our last spark of recognition, then I whisk away the photo Mike clings to, permanently severing our tie as I set him free.

Allowing myself to ascend toward the light, to possibilities, I let go....

CHAPTER 10

Twenty-five years into the future…

Emmie

The sunrise over the Black Hills sets my heart pounding as I rotate the closed sign to open. I learn each day is a blessing, as apparent by the seedlings that burst through the soil, flowering after I only planted them in the window boxes eight weeks ago. But what I need is a miracle to fix the broken lock, so I can officially open.

If the new owner of Deadwood Keys and Locks doesn't arrive in the next five minutes, opening day and the ribbon cutting ceremony will be ruined.

Customers can always come through the rear of the building, which used to be my grandmother's antique store, but my mom taught me that entering the back of the building on opening day is a bad omen, and I respect the woman.

Through the single-pane storefront glass, I spot Mom, but not Grandma. She's not as spry as she once was, walking with a cane now. But I know she's as excited about opening day as I am. "Mom, where's grandma?"

"In the back. She's setting up the coffee station."

Butterflies flit around the poppies, and, if I'm honest, inside my belly. It's a big decision to open a nursery/coffeehouse in Deadwood, but I'm home for good, after getting my master's in business, along with a BS in horticulture. Mom's moved her breakfast/coffeehouse business, combining our specialties into one big family affair. "And Dad? How are the pastries looking?"

A clatter of metal on concrete jolts me, and I suspect one of the serving trays has hurled itself off the table.

"Noel, you better come help before I make a mess of these scones."

Shaking my head, I don't blame Dad's unsteady hands. He's worried, but Mom knows him best. It's a big step for them to let go of their baby girl, but I'm ready to take on the world.

At least, I will be as soon as the locksmith arrives. I peer into the keyhole, spotting the broken-off iron key. One twist, and *snap*. The morning hinges on ruin if I don't open the front door.

Honk, honk.

The flower delivery truck pulls up to the curb, blossoms of all kinds and colors waiting to be unloaded. "Where do you want these, Emmie?"

I poke my head inside the passenger side of the truck, finding it empty. "Where's your help, Charlie? The store opens"—I check my watch—"in five minutes."

"Just me today. I should be able to unload these at the curb in twenty minutes."

My blood pressure jumps, and suddenly a headache screws behind my eyes. "I don't have twenty minutes. I need these inside and on the display benches."

"I have another delivery…" He begins by pulling down the tailgate and removing a single flat.

At this rate, we'll be here all day. "Take what you can around back."

Charlie's uniform is starched as usual and he's always pristine. Even his white truck is spotless and the flowers stacked and arranged by color. At least the nursery owner is fit—and I do appreciate the delivery.

My life's hanging in the balance as a first impression is everything. I want the nursery to boast life, the perfect Lyffe—my birth mom's last name. I even named the shop after her, after Noel's insistence. A Perfect Lyffe—Coffee, Flour & Flowers

I glance upward, sending a little prayer. "This is for you, Mom. I hope I make you proud."

The purr of a motorcycle rolls up beside me, but I don't have time to look as I hop up into the truck and grab one of the flats, plants blocking my view.

"Let me help you—"

"Oh!" I'm free falling, but then strong arms gather me up a millisecond before I slam onto the concrete curb. I'm shaking from embarrassment as I peer over the pansies.

But that's when I see him—*him*, like something straight out of a biker magazine.

His arms are inked in tribal markings, American

Indians, and wolves, all in full color. I'm biting my lip before I can stop myself, and his purple eyes remind me of Larkspurs, a flowering plant that's as tough and hardy as him. "I'm a lucky girl."

"I'm a lucky guy. I didn't figure the owner was on the menu when I rode up." He pushes out my hair that's intruding into his mouth with his tongue.

Of course, he's talking about my auburn hair that's refusing his efforts.

I scramble out of his arms, wiping away my strands while he takes the flat. "I'm sorry. I'm rushing, inviting disaster when I shouldn't be. The front door to my shop is jammed, since I broke the key inside the lock last night. I left a message with the new locksmith, but I'm not certain he received it. The chamber of commerce will be here anytime for the ribbon cutting, but I'm not sure what I'm going to do if I can't let customers inside."

He sets the flat on the bench. One by one, he loads the bench with multiple flats, and, when Charlie returns from taking his flat around the back, the stranger holds up a single finger, and the man freezes.

The power inside that motion does things to my belly I never allowed to blossom. I waited, never satisfied with guys my age, when I want a man.

Only the more I scrutinize the biker, I realize he has a familiarity that speaks to me. His hair is clipped tight to his head, but if he grew it out, it would be long and thick. I imagine what his hair would feel like running through my fingers. His nose isn't perfect, nor are his ears, and I wonder if he's been a fighter. But I don't care, not when he stalks toward me, pinning me with his thirsty stare.

"I-I need my door unlocked." OMG. "I mean, would you know how to pick a lock?"

"I can try…"

His breath is minty and hot, ramping up my attraction. "Please, hurry. Time is winding down fast."

In the saddlebag of his bike, he pulls out a ring, old keys hanging off the round. "One of these will do the trick."

There are skeleton keys, paracentric ones, and keys with decorative rings. "How can you be so sure one will fit? The lock is heart-shaped and unusual. If your key doesn't work, do you have a saw inside your pack? We may need to cut the door in half."

"No saw, but I can take the door off the hinges if I have to."

"You can take the door off my hinges," I mumble.

"What?"

"Nothing."

I almost kick myself into focusing on the task at hand when a line begins to form, murmurs crowding on my nerves. I raise both hands, patting the air. "We'll be opening as soon as the chamber arrives. I hope you're all hungry."

"I'm hungry, but it's not for breakfast."

I don't think I hear him right, but then the broken iron piece clings to the ground. He sifts through his assortment, holding up what looks like a match. Carefully, he inserts a key into the lock and turns, and the heart-shaped latch sails open.

I spring into his arms, and he should push me away, but he doesn't. "You saved the day. You're my hero!"

"What are locksmiths for, but unlocking hearts?"

I catch Noel inside, a wide-ass smile on her face as she clutches her crystal pendant.

And I wonder if fate is working here, or a dash of magic when I feel as if I waited for a feeling, a sign, and he's standing before me. But what if I'm being wishful, silly, gullible Emmie listening to her family stories…? "I guess we should talk about payment."

He lands his lips on mine without permission, but full of purpose. And I open for him, drawing him in, tasting, devouring this man who feels more familiar than my left hand is to my right. And I consider if grand possibilities wait for me.

"You're beautiful, deadly, captivating," he purrs against my lips. "I'm a *very* lucky man."

Lowering his head, he reclaims my mouth, each cheek, my neck, sucking and grinding his stubble against my sensitive skin and drawing a moan out of me right here on Main Street for the world to see. I won't deny his magical touch revs my desire until I'm wet with an unrelenting need. I want him inside of me in a desperate way, and, as I stare into his darkening eyes, I think he hungers for me, too.

Static sparks as we sandwich my locket between us, a locket he takes up into his thick fingers, reading the inscription.

"Well, well, well… 'Claimed by the Outlaw.' Now that's what I'm talking about. But I'm not interested in possessing anyone. Forever is our playground. And this devil is going to play hard, soon as you say so."

I gasp, the baritone of his voice heavy with want and thick with need, yet tinted by reservation and respect. And something else—a lost memory or a promise. But am I ready? "I have a shop to open."

"I'll stick around, in case you want anything else revealed, but first, tell me your name."

Mom and Dad are church mice, and grandma's blotting her eyes. But the day they presented me with the locket, a choice to accept fate existed, along with possibilities of something out of my control, someone who searches for me. They clued me in that this day might come. A stranger who feels as familiar as my heartbeat waiting for me to need him, to crave him, to want him forever. I waited. I'm ready. It was my mom's final words, her final declaration, and I recall her mention of a soulmate, as if her memories are my own.

Jump in. Head first. Never look back.

So, I do. "I'm Emmie."

He sets me down and picks up the bench, motioning to Charlie to take up the other end. The duo hauls the delivery inside in the nick of time.

But an uncanny feeling overwhelms me, assuring me this man will wait a lifetime for me. I believe with all my heart that we'll be together even longer. And when he takes me up in his arms as I cut the red ribbon, carrying me over the threshold, he kisses me long and hard, until I feel...claimed. Until I feel absolutely at peace. Until I feel loved.

"You didn't tell me *your* name."

Against my lips, he breathes, "You always call me James."

The End

* * *

**If you enjoyed this story,
please consider leaving a review.**

Ready for more fated mate stories like this? Read the completed Faeted Vampire series, where a hidden fae princess with untamed powers and a vampire who thirsts for her blood must combine forces to destroy a dark supernatural force in time to save their second chance at love?

Find all of Cyndi's books and never miss a release, sign up for Cyndi's newsletter and receive a free digital book at www.cyndifaria.com.

About the Author, Cyndi Faria

Two-Time *USA Today* Bestselling Author of The Faeted Vampire Series, Cyndi Faria writes steamy paranormal vampire, werewolf & shifter romance with twist-turns you'll never see coming and happily ever after endings you crave.

Twilight fan extraordinaire, she fell in love with vampire fated mates and #TeamEdward, but always wondered, what if Bella chose #TeamJacob, the Alpha furry option, instead?

Paranormal fated mates Fifty Shades style and worlds infused with dark magic have been this authors passion since.

When this California girl isn't nose-deep in new adult & college fantasy romance, she's snuggling on the couch with her rescued fur babies, sipping tea, and binging on Vampire Diaries reruns or her guilty pleasure, The Bachelor!

Subscribe to Cyndi Faria's newsletter for a free digital book to get started on at www.cyndifaria.com.

Connect with Cyndi

Cyndi loves to hear from readers!

Want to be the first to know about Cover Reveals, New Releases, Excerpts, and Giveaways, sign up for Cyndi's newsletter and get a free digital book: www.cyndifaria.com

Facebook: www.facebook.com/cyndifariaauthor
Twitter: @cyndifaria
Instagram: @Cyndi Faria
Pinterest: Cyndi Faria Author
TikTok: @cyndifariaauthor

"(Cyndi Faria) has a talent for lovely happy endings and I'm so glad she does." ~Night Owl Reviews